"Will you marry me, Wade? Will you be my husband?"

Wade sucked in his breath. "You think it's possible to put all the agony of the past behind us?"

"Yes!" Janet blurted. "Don't you?"

His eyes continued to penetrate hers, but they were full of doubts. "I'm not sure."

Swallowing hard, she said "Remember I told you that if the day ever came when you wanted to talk to me, I would be here waiting for you." Her voice wobbled. "As you can see, I'm still here. You do love me, don't you?"

He raked his unsteady hands through his hair. "That's not the point, Janet."

"Then what is?"

True love is worth waiting for...

Dear Reader,

Harlequin Romance® is delighted to invite you to another
WHITE WEDDING.

Everyone loves a wedding with all the excitement of the
big day: flowers, champagne and the thrill of a happy
couple exchanging vows. But these blushing brides and
gorgeous grooms have chosen to make their day
extraspecial.

For better or worse, they are determined the bride should
wear white on her wedding day—which means keeping
passions in check! Because for these couples, true love
waits.

Happy Reading!

The Editors

THE FAITHFUL BRIDE

Rebecca Winters

WHITE
WEDDINGS

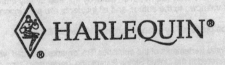

HARLEQUIN®

TORONTO • NEW YORK • LONDON
AMSTERDAM • PARIS • SYDNEY • HAMBURG
STOCKHOLM • ATHENS • TOKYO • MILAN • MADRID
PRAGUE • WARSAW • BUDAPEST • AUCKLAND

ISBN 0-373-03617-5

THE FAITHFUL BRIDE

First North American Publication 2000.

Copyright © 2000 by Rebecca Winters.

Visit us at www.eHarlequin.com

Printed in U.S.A.

CHAPTER ONE

"I STILL don't feel right about leaving you alone over the holiday, darling. Why don't you come to Hawaii with your father and me? You haven't had a vacation since you went to Florida with Annabelle two years ago."

Janet Larson loved her mother for caring about her, but she hated it when those deep blue eyes the exact color of her own took on that haunted look. At times like this she knew exactly what her parent was thinking.

It's not fair that my daughter's best friend is married, and I'm going on a second honeymoon when she hasn't been on her first one yet.

"In case you've forgotten, Mom, I haven't lived at home for years, and it's not *my* holiday. I'm not a mother and probably never will be one. I think it was sweet of Dad to plan a second honeymoon for the two of you. I'll call you at your hotel on Mother's Day."

Janet handed her elegant, statuesque parent a gaily wrapped gift to put in her suitcase. She'd combed every exclusive store in Salt Lake until she'd found the right taupe-colored bag in expensive leather.

"I know you wanted a son-in-law for Mother's Day," she muttered, "but once again I have to disappoint you. What a shame you and Dad couldn't have had more children who would have provided you with some grandchildren by now."

Her mother acted as if she'd just been slapped. "I've never said that to you!"

Janet flashed her a teasing smile. "I know. You're the antithesis of Jane Austen's Mrs. Bennett. For a mother with only one child who happens to be a thirty-year-old unmarried female, you should receive an award for being the least meddlesome parent on the planet.

"But, Mom, I *feel* your pain. That's why I brought up the subject. We need to talk about it once and for all, and then forget it. The point is, I love my life just the way it is. Be happy for me! I have a wonderful family and friends, a fascinating career. I date men I find attractive. Maybe one day I'll fall in love, but so far it hasn't happened."

"Because you *won't* allow it to happen?"

Janet's adrenaline surged. "What do you mean?"

"I'm talking about Wade, of course."

After all this time, just hearing her mother say his name out loud sent a stabbing pain to her heart. "That was ten years ago."

"Forty years ago, I fell madly in love with your father. Sometimes I think you and I have a lot more in common than our looks." The two women could be twins except that Janet's shoulder-length hair didn't have a trace of gray among the glossy black strands. "You wouldn't by any chance be waiting for him to come back?"

"*What?*" Heat filled Janet's cheeks. "How can you even ask me a question like that?"

"I'm not saying it's a conscious wish on your part, darling. What I do believe is that when he never returned from Colorado and broke things off over the phone, you never fully recovered. Maybe you ought to seek professional counseling so you can get past this and allow yourself to fall in love with someone else.''

Janet blinked. "You're serious."

Her mom put an arm around her shoulders. "For a beautiful young woman who dates as often as you do, doesn't it strike you as odd that in ten years you've never gotten involved with another man?"

"I've been too busy establishing my career."

Her mother eyed her shrewdly before letting out a resigned sigh. "You're the one who wanted to talk. But evidently it's still too painful." After letting go of her, she closed the lid of the suitcase. "For once I believe I'm going to be ready when your father gets here."

Janet wished she'd never broached the subject of her single status. The conversation had brought up too many painful memories lying dormant.

"I hope you have a wonderful trip in Hawaii with Dad. Don't open my present until Sunday. I'll see you when you get back next Friday."

Suspiciously bright blue eyes stared back at her. "I still wish you were coming with us."

"I couldn't leave if I wanted to. At the moment, I'm knee-deep in three bankruptcy cases, and I have an important meeting with a client in South Salt Lake in half an hour. As it is, I'm going to be late." She gave her mother a hug and kiss. "That's for Dad, too," she whispered before hurrying out of her parents' home.

As she zoomed away in the blue convertible she'd bought used, she realized that if she didn't have to obey the traffic laws, she could make her meeting at Recreational Outdoor Equipment with time to spare.

However, after passing the bar several years back, she'd sworn an oath before the chief justice of the supreme court of Utah to uphold all the laws in her capacity as an attorney. That meant slowing down to a comfortable twelve miles over the speed limit.

Needing a distraction, she turned on her favorite classical music station. *Tannhäuser*. Wagner's surging music fitted her mood as she passed one car after another along the interstate at the base of the mountains. They looked quite magnificent today against the brilliant blue May sky. With the unseasonably hot weather, she'd been able to put the top down. The feel of the wind tossing her hair gave her the added sense of freedom she needed right now to vent her chaotic emotions.

Normally she kept Wade in a private compartment of her heart that she rarely opened. She had only herself to blame if she was suffering now. Maybe her mother was right. It was more than possible she needed outside help to exorcise him from her consciousness.

That was what it was going to take.

Total eradication.

But right now, her first priority was to concentrate on her client, Mr. Loomis. If at all possible, she would help him to avoid bankruptcy. Last week, she'd asked him to make out a budget with his accountant to give her some idea if he could pay off his debts within three years. Depending on what she found out in this meeting, she would know whether or not he had to file for Chapter Eleven bankruptcy.

Janet tried to approach every case as if the problem were happening to her. Personalizing it often forced her to figure out ways to turn things around. Nothing made her feel better than to prevent someone in the business world from going under financially. Each victory supplied absolution from the guilt she carried around for having been blessed with so much materially while others struggled to make ends meet.

Larson Oil, of which her father was president, had been a family-run company for three generations. As her parents' only child, she'd been given the benefit of the best of everything, even to graduating with honors from Stanford Law School.

After leaving California, she'd returned to Salt Lake where she'd been asked to join a prestigious law firm, all because of family connections, though the head of the firm swore otherwise. She now had her own office with secretary and was making a six figure salary.

It didn't seem fair that lucrative investments were growing for her future, while Mr. Loomis was fighting for survival. All men might be created equal, but for an act of birth, life didn't give equally of its abundance. There needed to be a better way to distribute the wealth. Since law school, she'd given the problem a lot of thought. But right now, she needed to come up with a plan so her client wouldn't lose his shirt.

Two minutes before the meeting was due to start, she pulled into a parking space in front of ROE. Taking advantage of the time, she touched up her lipstick and brushed her hair. Like her mother, she was lucky to have natural curl. No matter how messy it got, she could repair the damage easily enough.

Reaching across to the passenger side of the car, she grabbed the expensive brown leather briefcase with the gold initials her father had given her when she'd passed the bar, then hurried inside the building.

From the huge amount of inventory, not to mention the crush of customers, it looked like ROE enjoyed a thriving business. But she knew differently as she headed for the main office at the rear of the store.

The college-aged woman at the counter got off the phone when she saw her coming. "Can I help you?"

"Yes. Would you tell Mr. Loomis that Janet Larson is here. He's expecting me."

"The meeting has already started. Go right on in. He's the first door on the left."

Already started? How could the meeting have started without *her*?

Giving the receptionist a thank you, she headed down the hall. The door stood ajar. Through the aperture, Mr. Loomis saw her and got to his feet.

"Come in, Ms. Larson."

Janet entered the room. A chair had been placed opposite his desk for her. Two other men who'd already been seated around him rose to their feet.

"Ms. Larson? May I present Mr. Bart Sims, an attorney from Denver."

From Denver? She automatically put out her hand to greet the sandy-haired lawyer, but her gaze went beyond him to lock with a pair of silvery-gray eyes she could never forget in a millennium.

Those were the eyes that had haunted her for the past ten years, but in her dreams they'd blazed with desire for her, not accusation.

She gasped before the room began to reel. Invisible bands constricted her chest so she couldn't breathe.

Wade.

When had he come back to Salt Lake?

Was it a total coincidence that her mother had brought up his name today? Or had she already heard from someone that he was in town?

Except for his eyes, everything else about him had changed since she'd last seen him. In college he'd been a lean, six-foot-two male with short-cropped brown hair. Ten years had added bulk and muscle to make him a powerful-looking man.

He wore his wavy hair longer now. It suited his rugged features. Lines of experience around his straight nose and compelling mouth gave character to an unforgettable face that had grown even more handsome with the passage of time.

The tiny scar at the bottom of his chin received from a skiing accident was barely noticeable anymore. The tip of her ski pole had accidentally broken the skin when they'd both fallen in the snow during a run at Snowbird, one of Utah's ski resorts. The little faded mark reminded her of the many times she'd brushed her lips against his face and neck and mouth and scar as a prelude to his kissing them both into oblivion.

She saw something else that made her feel so ill she needed to sit down.

A gold wedding band adorned his ring finger.

He was married. Of course he would be. He probably had children. She groaned inwardly.

"And allow me to introduce Mr. Wade Holt. He represen—"

"We've met," Wade interjected without shaking her

hand. The deep masculine voice she'd loved so well held no warmth, killing her a little more.

Obeying a compulsion she couldn't help, she glanced at him with wounded eyes if only to reassure herself that she wasn't in the middle of an agonizing dream. A wintry expression along with some other emotion she couldn't define was still there in those stormy depths as he stared back at her. It left her feeling so hollow inside she wanted to die.

Mr. Loomis cleared his throat. "Ms. Larson? As you know, I engaged a Realtor to help find a buyer for the company before I realized how much trouble I was in. After I retained you, Mr. Holt here, the owner and CEO of Rocky Mountain Enterprises, contacted me with an offer to pay off the creditors and take over the company. Under the circumstances, I'm going to do business with him and thought you could act as my attorney to handle the legal matters."

Then you've thought wrong, Mr. Loomis.

If Janet recalled correctly, Rocky Mountain Enterprises had its corporate headquarters in Denver, Colorado, but they did a lot of business out of state.

Word had it among Utah financiers in the upper echelons that the growing Denver business concern enjoyed the enviable reputation of buying struggling businesses and turning them around before selling them to the tune of millions of dollars in profits. To think it was Wade's company...

I've got to get out of here.

She fought to keep her poise. "Since you've decided to sell, then you need the services of a good corporate attorney." Her client sat there looking stunned, but she couldn't help it. There was no way in this world she could stay in there another minute. "I can give you the names of several excellent lawyers who handle these transactions as a matter of course."

Her hand shook as she reached in the briefcase for her notepad and jotted down three different law firms. Praying she wouldn't faint before she left the room, she got to her feet and put the paper on his desk.

"There you go. Any one of them will do a fine job for you. Mr. Loomis, gentlemen?" she said, feeling distinctly light-headed, "it's been a pleasure."

Somehow she made it out of the room and the building. But by the time she reached her car, she couldn't hold back the devastating pain of Wade's repudiation. After sliding behind the wheel, she collapsed in a paroxysm of tears, mindless of any onlookers.

It had taken her years to finally accept the fact that he'd fallen out of love with her. But a decade had gone by since then. No matter his personal feelings when he'd left the state, how could he have treated her so coldly just now? Those arctic eyes froze her out as if she were something unpleasant he would willingly crush under his heel.

After a few more minutes, she pulled herself together enough to reach for the cell phone and punch in her best friend's number. It didn't surprise her when she got her voice mail. No doubt Annabelle Dunbarton, a crack P.I. with the Lufka Private Detective Agency, was out on a case with her husband, Rand.

"I need to talk to you, Annie. This is really important." Her voice shook. "Give me a call whenever you can."

Needing her friend as never before, she sped out of the parking lot toward the freeway, anxious to put as many miles as she could between herself and the man she still loved with all her heart and soul.

Damn, damn, damn.

"Luanne?"

Wade's pleasant, unflappable, middle-aged secretary lifted her head in surprise. "Mr. Holt—you're back! I thought you were going to be in Salt Lake for the rest of the week."

So did I.

"Something came up. Until further notice, pretend I'm still gone."

"Yes, sir."

His proposed three-day trip had lasted all of six hours. *Hell.*

After shutting the door to his private office, he took off his coat and tie, undid the top buttons of his shirt, then poured himself a Scotch from the minibar his secretary kept stocked for clients.

A stack of new correspondence sat on his desk. He riffled through the pile with disinterest, but one envelope marked Personal caught his attention. When he opened it, he discovered the wedding announcement of his ex-wife Claire.

She'd written an accompanying note.

Wade?

Since you don't always check the mail right away when you're home, I wanted to be sure you got this before someone else told you about it first. I love Paul very much.

I just hope that one day you'll find the happiness you couldn't find with me.

Love, Claire.

Wade swallowed his drink in one gulp.

He'd been praying for this day since their divorce three years ago. The relief from guilt was almost as exquisite as his pain over seeing Janet again.

When Loomis told him they were waiting for his attorney, Wade had no idea Janet would come walking through that door.

Dear God. She'd always been a beautiful girl, the kind you expected to win the Miss America Pageant. Ten years had only managed to turn her into an even more gorgeous woman.

He could have guessed she'd become an attorney. Janet had always been a brilliant student with the kind of intelligence to forge a career in any field she chose.

But he'd expected Mr. Loomis to introduce her as Mrs. Clark and was stunned to discover that she still went by the name Larson.

He wondered if she had ended up marrying Ty, yet used her maiden name for business. A lot of female attorneys did that these days. The fact that he hadn't seen a wedding ring on her finger didn't mean anything. She'd never been able to tolerate jewelry.

Once when he'd asked her to wear his fraternity ring until he could afford an engagement ring, she'd had to refuse him. Apparently her skin was too sensitive to metal and broke out in hives. On the night of the winter fest party, when the fraternity had made her their sweetheart for the year, he'd pinned her instead. But he imagined she'd long since thrown it away along with everything else he'd ever given her after she'd decided she wanted Ty.

Wade had to admit it gave him a perverse sense of pleasure to witness her hasty exit from Loomis's office. After she had betrayed Wade all those years ago, it came as a surprise that she would still be uncomfortable in the same room with him. He figured any woman who didn't know the meaning of love had no compunctions whatsoever.

In fact, he was still in shock that she recognized him, let alone that she'd stared back at him out of dark-fringed blue eyes shadowed by what looked like pain.

He had to have been mistaken about that.

When it came to pain, she didn't have an inkling.

The second she'd left the room, Loomis apologized profusely for wasting Wade's time. But Wade told him not to worry about it.

Pretending that his life hadn't been turned inside out, he defended Janet by telling Loomis she'd done the right thing to excuse herself from a business transaction that no longer needed a bankruptcy attorney. He suggested that the other man phone one of the law firms she'd noted on the paper. When another meeting was set up, Wade and Bart would fly to Salt Lake again. No harm done.

No harm done.

Lord. His eyes closed tightly.

Over the past two years he'd been to Salt Lake on

business dozens of times. Returning to the scene of the crime hadn't turned out to be the traumatizing experience he'd expected and feared. In fact, just last year he'd congratulated himself for having successfully buried the past altogether.

Like hell!

"Luanne?"

"Yes, Mr. Holt?"

"I'm headed for the gym. Call Mr. Harsh and reschedule him to meet with me at nine in the morning instead of next week."

"I'll try, but I think he might have gone on vacation."

"See what you can do."

"Certainly."

He shoved himself away from the desk. Right now, he was feeling intensely physical. A workout wouldn't solve what was wrong with him, but for the moment he couldn't think of anything else that would prevent him from going over the edge.

Janet Larson was beautifully alive and doing well. A phone call away...

The knowledge flung him back into the recurring nightmare that had destroyed his marriage. According to Claire, theirs hadn't been a true marriage. It was more a ménage à trois, with Janet being the invisible third party.

Though he'd done everything in his power to be a good husband, deep in his gut Wade knew Claire's accusation was true. Janet had worked her way so tightly into his psyche, he'd never been able to shake her loose.

The first day of his senior year of high school when she'd walked into the chemistry class, he caught one glimpse of the statuesque, black-haired beauty and couldn't take his eyes off her. As she'd looked around for an empty seat at one of the tables in the crowded room, their gazes collided. Those impossibly dark blue orbs caused an emotional stir that left him breathless.

He'd had crushes on other girls before in Denver but knew this time it was different.

Since his parents' divorce, he'd come to live temporarily with his father in Salt Lake and didn't know many students except for the guys he'd been working out with on the football team over the summer. He leaned over to ask one of the fullbacks who she was.

"If you're talking about Wonder Woman over there, you can forget it. Janet Larson doesn't date football players. She comes from big money. Ever heard of Larson Oil?"

"Of course."

"With her brains, she doesn't need the bucks. She'll get a fully paid scholarship to Wellesley or Vassar back East after graduation. In case you were getting any ideas, she only dates guys with four point averages."

"How do you know that?" Wade persisted.

"Because most of the guys on the team have tried. She brushes us all off."

"Does she have a boyfriend?"

"She dates Ty Clark, the governor's son."

"I heard he's the new president of the school."

"Yeah. He's also president of the debate club. She's one of the top debaters in the region. Ty'll be going to Yale or Princeton or some posh university next year. They'll probably end up getting married."

"That's interesting," Wade murmured, but his thoughts were racing ahead.

As soon as class was over, he headed down to the counselor's office and made arrangements to check into the debate class. The only one taught started at seven-thirty in the morning. He had to drop a quantum physics class in order to take it. But that was all right. He would sign up for it the third trimester after football was over.

Before he went to practice that afternoon, he stopped by the debate coach's room, introduced himself and asked for a disclosure so he'd be prepared for class the next day.

After football, he went to the main public library. Until the doors closed, he did research on the current debate topic about the pros and cons of the nuclear arms dilemma. Feeling that he was as equipped as any other student on the subject after a first day, he showed up early for class the next morning.

When Janet Larson entered the room, she must have recognized Wade from the day before because she smiled at him. Up close, she was even more breathtaking than he'd realized. His heart did a wild kick before he smiled back and asked her to sit by him.

After they'd introduced themselves, she said, "You're new here."

"That's right." He had a hard time concentrating as he admired her shapely body and long, slender legs. "I'm from Denver. My parents' divorced last spring. After talking it over with my mom, I decided to live with my dad for a year and go home for holidays."

With those revelations, her expressive blue eyes suddenly darkened with compassion. "I—I can't imagine my parents divorcing," she said quietly. "You must be in a lot of pain."

The sincerity in her voice reached a secret part of him. He found himself telling her things he rarely admitted to anyone.

"I was at first, but I'm getting used to it. I miss my mother, but she's got a good job as a nurse and has my two younger sisters to worry about. Right now, I feel like my dad needs me more. He's a reformed alcoholic who's lost more jobs than you can count. Now he's trying to build a new life."

The bell had rung, but the class was still filling up and the teacher hadn't come in yet.

Her haunted gaze searched his. "Do you live close to the school?"

He nodded. "In those apartments on the hill above the tennis courts. It helps because I don't have a car."

He watched her digest that information. After a slight hesitation, she said, "I know a lot of kids who ride bikes everywhere."

Because he'd learned about the kind of monied background she came from, her sensitivity on the subject surprised and touched him.

"That's how I get to my job."

"What do you do?"

He didn't feel that she was patronizing him. On the contrary, she sounded like she really wanted to know.

"I wait tables at El Gaucho's three nights a week."

"When do you plan to do your homework?"

"Over the years, I've learned that most of the time I can get it done in class while I'm waiting for something to happen."

She knew exactly what he meant. Their debate coach hadn't shown up yet.

When she broke into that full-bodied smile once more, it felt like the rush he got during a downhill ski run in Breckenridge where you started at eleven thousand feet and shushed a nearly vertical drop to the base several thousand feet below.

"Have you taken debate before, Janet?"

"Yes. I love it. What about you?"

"This will be my first experience. Since you're a pro, what do I need to know right off?"

"I'm no expert," she denied modestly as the teacher entered the room.

"Good morning, class! Sorry I'm late. We have a new student today. Wade Holt? Stand up. He hails from Denver, Colorado. Welcome to the jungle."

Everyone laughed and clapped except for a nice-looking, dark blond guy wearing preppy clothes and sitting two chairs away. He'd been scowling at Wade for the past couple of minutes. His identity wasn't in question. Ty Clark had president of the student body written all over him.

"For the first time in three years, our class is made up of an even number of males and females. Therefore I'm going to mix up the teams for this trimester. Wade? Since you're already sitting by Janet, I'll put you two together. Annabelle, you'll join Ty."

Wade saw the cute redhead seated on Janet's other side whisper something to her.

The teacher continued to pair off her class.

Things couldn't have turned out better if Wade had orchestrated them himself. The only person in the room

Wade cared about seemed to be equally happy with the arrangement. Maybe Janet wasn't as interested in Ty Clark as his football buddy had assumed.

As far as Wade was concerned, the president of the school could take a flying leap.

The teacher hadn't finished giving instructions. "Janet, Jah-Jun and Moonerah's teams will take the affirmative side, the rest of you the negative. I gave out disclosures yesterday, so you know the question and you've seen the dates for the various tournaments. Get busy in your groups making an outline of how you plan to proceed. I want those on my desk before you leave class today."

Wade took the paper from his notebook that contained the notes he'd made from his research the night before. He put them on Janet's desk.

After studying them for a moment, she lifted her head with its mane of glossy black hair and stared at him in stunned surprise. "You said you hadn't debated before."

"I haven't. Since I was a day late for class, I thought I'd better come with something to offer."

"Something to offer?" she blurted. "This is outstanding. You have solid documentation here on both sides of the issue that couldn't have come off the Internet because I've already checked." Her blue eyes blazed with new light.

"The Net can be entertaining, but I don't use it for anything academic unless I already know the source is legitimate."

"Neither do I. Anyone can create a Web page claiming to be an expert."

"With this kind of a question, we probably need to interview live sources."

She nodded excitedly. "Senator Marsh lives around the corner from my house. I'm pretty sure we can make arrangements to talk to him before we have to attend our first debate tournament in two weeks. What nights are you free?"

"Don't worry about that," he said, trying to smother his elation that there was going to be a next time for the two of them outside of school. "If he's willing to talk to us, I'll work around his schedule."

Too soon the period ended. At that point, Janet introduced him to her best friend, Annabelle. The vivacious redhead was the one to pry it out of him that he was number fifty-seven on the football team. Since she loved the game, she said that she and Janet would be at the next one to cheer him on.

"That's very nice, but don't come for my sake. I arrived midsummer from out of state, which makes me third string. I'll probably sit on the bench most of the season," he admitted candidly.

Out of the corner of his eyes, he could see Ty at the door, no doubt waiting for Janet to join him.

"That's cruel when you go to all those practices and suit up," she said unexpectedly. Again he felt Janet's concern. It was a revelation to him considering her privileged lifestyle.

He grinned. "That's football. I still have fun. Well, I guess I'll see you tomorrow."

Wade had no idea how he was going to make it through the next twenty-four hours until he could be with her again. By the end of the week they'd both fallen in love. When Wade asked her about Ty Clark, she said they'd been friends since grade school. Though they'd attended several dances together, it meant nothing. Wade believed her, and it was all he needed to hear.

Eight months later, Janet could have had her pick of three Ivy League universities or the University of Utah to attend on full scholarship. She chose the latter to be with Wade.

Apparently Ty decided not to leave the state, either. He ended up in the same fraternity as Wade, who by this time needed a place to live on campus. His father had made another move back to Denver to try to reconcile with Wade's mother.

One weekend in mid-January, Wade went home to tell his parents he was going to marry Janet. She'd already met his dad, but Wade wanted his mom to invite her to Denver so the whole family could meet and make plans for the wedding.

With everything arranged, he flew back to Salt Lake a day early because he was missing her too much and wanted to surprise her. But after he tried to phone her from the fraternity house to tell her he had returned, he learned something about Janet and Ty that destroyed his world forever.

The pain was so excruciating, he packed up his personal belongings and headed back to Denver on the next flight. Two days later, he phoned Janet and told her he'd had second thoughts about getting married. For a variety of reasons, not the least of which was the disparity in their backgrounds, he didn't think a marriage between them would work out after all.

For the next five weeks she phoned him every day, sobbing. But no amount of begging or pleading reached him.

Finally she told him she wouldn't bother him anymore. But if the day ever came that he wanted to talk to her, she would be there waiting for him because there would never be another man for her.

Such a superb actress...

That was the last memory he had of his sweet, brilliant, noble, virtuous, *treacherous* fiancée.

Now a new memory supplanted the old.

Most people were never given a second chance to go back and deal with their nemesis, to tear it apart layer by layer, to dissect it until it was all laid out on the table wounded and bleeding. By some quirk of fate, he'd been handed that rare opportunity today, but he'd let her slip away.

He could still take advantage of it if he wanted to. All he had to do was get on another plane....

CHAPTER TWO

"Ms. LARSON? There's a Mr. Holt in reception who would like to see you. He doesn't have an appointment. When I told him you were busy with another client, he said he would wait no matter how long it took. What do you want me to do?"

Annabelle had warned Janet she probably hadn't seen the last of Wade, not after the way she'd left Mr. Loomis without an attorney last week. In case Wade decided to catch up with her, Janet ought to be happy for the chance to see him again. Enough time had gone by that he would probably answer her specific questions. Annabelle felt a meeting between the two of them would be the best thing in the world for Janet so she could lay the past to rest.

They were both adults now with important careers and responsibilities. On top of that, Wade was a married man. Surely at this point, he and Janet could have a dispassionate conversation about why he'd really broken off with her and left Salt Lake for good.

"Give me two more minutes, then send him in, Sandy."

"Okay."

Janet had taken off her navy suit jacket to work on some briefs. But knowing Wade was about to enter her domain, she slipped it back on over her white silk blouse with the red and blue print to present a more formal

26

appearance. She decided not to refurbish her lipstick. The last thing she wanted was for him to think she was worried about her looks.

Heavens! There'd been a time years ago when she'd done everything in her power to make herself so beautiful he would never want to look at anyone else. But she still hadn't been able to hold on to him.

What a fool she'd been to think Wade was different from all other boys who at the tender age of twenty were generally too immature to know what they wanted out of life, let alone *whom* they wanted as a lifetime companion.

Janet's parents tended to believe that explanation best explained his defection, rather than his lame excuse about the differences in their social standing and economic backgrounds not boding well for marriage. He was too young and had gotten in too deep, her father had said. Not knowing how to pull out gracefully, he'd done the cowardly thing in the end and run away, unable to face her.

It made a lot of sense if Janet applied that scenario to anyone but Wade. Somehow she hadn't bought it then and didn't buy it now. Annabelle hadn't been persuaded by that argument, either, but she'd never been able to offer another one that made more sense.

Perhaps the next few minutes would verify that her parents' theory had been right after all. If that were the case, then it meant Janet had an adult case of arrested development and really did need professional help.

Her door had been left ajar. She felt his presence before she lifted her head and watched him walk into her office dressed in an expensive-looking, double-breasted gray suit with a charcoal shirt and print tie.

He'd always portrayed a confidence she knew other boys envied and girls admired. Now that he'd matured into a striking thirty-year-old man, he had an additional air of authority and substance that made him a powerful figure to reckon with. He shut the door, sealing them inside.

"Hello, Wade." Thank heaven her voice remained steady. "I didn't expect to see you again, but since you're in Salt Lake and have taken the trouble to come by my office, please sit down."

"Thank you." He subsided into one of the leather chairs placed opposite her walnut desk. In one sweeping gaze he'd made an assessment of the dark-stained paneling and shelves of law books.

"No personal pictures besides your parents?"

He noticed everything.

"No." Her voice quavered. *Damn*. Every memory of him lay in a box she hadn't opened in years.

"Your inner sanctum is very impressive, yet your choice of plants and paintings gives it the right feminine touch. You always did have exquisite taste."

That hurtful hint of mockery in his tone was deliberate. She couldn't believe the sophisticated man seated across from her was the same Wade who'd once been the center of her universe. How could he talk to her this way after all they'd shared?

"Thank you. Can I have my secretary bring you coffee or a drink of some kind?"

"I think not, but I appreciate the offer." The whole time they talked, his laser-like eyes probed hers.

Growing more and more wary, she asked quietly, "Did Mr. Loomis find another attorney?"

"He must have done. Bart and I have an appointment with him in an hour."

Wade lounged in his chair like some magnificent jungle cat. But the negative tension emanating from him was so strong she knew better than to be deceived by his seeming state of rest.

"You still don't wear jewelry." He inserted the observation, no doubt to plunge the knife a little deeper.

Dear God. How long did he intend this horrific journey down memory lane to continue? Why did he come if he didn't want to talk about Mr. Loomis?

"No," she managed to rally. "But I see you've acquired a wedding ring since the last time I saw you. D-do you have children?" she stammered. Just saying the word reopened a wound that had never healed. *And never would.*

"The baby we would've had died three months into Claire's pregnancy. After that experience, she didn't want to try again."

Janet couldn't prevent the gasp that escaped. The revelation brought on new degrees of pain. For him, because he'd always talked about having a family and would have been devastated by the miscarriage as much as his wife.

But Janet was devastated, too. Part of her dream had been to give Wade children. She couldn't count the number of times they'd talked about the family they would raise, the wonderful life they would have together loving and teaching their babies about the world.

No matter how much Wade had changed over the

years, she knew his desire to be a father would always remain a constant.

"I'm so sorry," she said in an agonized whisper.

He bit out an unintelligible oath, causing her whole body to tremble in alarm. His eyes had turned the color of thunderheads.

"Some things don't change. *Lord*. You're still the same consummate actress who knows how to inject just the right amount of pain and compassion to twist my guts inside out."

"*Wade...*"

Her outcry produced a smirk.

"Your figure is more stunning than ever. You'll always have that untouched quality about you even though we both know that's not the case."

His words sent her into shock.

No man had ever touched her but Wade. Though they'd come close to losing complete control many times, they'd stopped short of making love because they'd wanted their wedding night to really mean something. That was why they'd planned their marriage so soon into college, because they knew they couldn't hold out any longer.

Wade couldn't have forgotten about that!

So what did he mean by his innuendo?

"Tell me something," he continued in the same vein. "How many children are back at the mansion with a nanny in residence?"

His startling question brought her to her feet. She was trembling so hard she had to keep her hands on the table to support herself. "Whose children are you talking about?"

"Yours, of course" came the deceptively bland response.

She shook her head in despair. "I don't have any."

He sat back in the chair with a satisfied smile that chilled her by its lack of warmth. "You still have the power to surprise me even though I know our relationship was riddled with lies. Lovesick swain that I was, I bought every last one of them."

"What are you talking about?" she cried in an agonized whisper.

"The business about never putting a career before family, for instance."

"*What family?*" Her question reverberated in the room.

He sprang to his feet in one lithe movement. Lines she hadn't seen before darkened his handsome face, making him look older.

"I may be an anachronism, but when a man and woman marry, I still consider them a family."

"So do I!"

Only the depth of the desk separated them. This close, she saw something flicker in the recesses of those silvery-dark pools. It could signify anything. Her heart filled with fresh anguish.

"Maybe I had this all figured wrong. Are you telling me that you're divorced already?"

"*Divorced*? I've never been married! If someone gave you that information, then you were grossly misinformed!"

His mouth went white around the edges. "In other words, after you and Ty got what you wanted from each other, he decided he couldn't trust you, either, and moved on. Or was it the other way around and he was the beggar, but you'd already found someone else?''

''*What*?'' This time, her cry exploded in the room.

''Drop the act, Janet. I know it all,'' he said, his voice grating, ''but I want to hear it from those lips that used to promise me paradise on a regular basis. Why not come clean. They say confession cleanses the soul. How many Ty's have there been in your life since him?''

Had he really said what she thought he'd just said?

His off-the-wall assertions, not to mention erroneous conclusions about a past life she'd never lived, were too incredible, too ludicrous to entertain, let alone address. But as she stared into his accusing eyes and received the full impact of his outrage, she realized that *he* believed them.

Dear God.

The room started to spin.

She sank onto her chair once more, so shaken by this revelation she couldn't think with any coherence.

''Ms. Larson?'' her secretary's voice sounded unexpectedly over the intercom.

Struggling for breath, she said, ''Yes?''

''Mr. Booth is here.''

''A-ask him to wait. I'll see him in a few minutes.''

''Very well.''

''Far be it from me to interfere with your busy schedule,'' Wade muttered. ''I'll let myself out.''

''No! You can't go! Not yet!''

Afraid he would leave and she might never see him again, she leaped out of her chair and ran past him to block his exit from the room. Out of breath, her chest rose and fell, drawing his attention to her body flattened against the door to prevent his leaving. Maybe it was a trick of light, but for an instant she thought she saw hunger in his eyes as his gaze wandered over her in the old familiar way.

She could hardly swallow. "Ten years ago, you broke off our engagement without having the decency to face me. No matter how many times I begged you to come back or let me go there so we could talk, you shut me out and left me with no choice but to forget you. Now, suddenly, you show up at my office after all these years and make accusations about me and Ty I don't begin to comprehend."

The tears had started flowing. She didn't know how to stop them.

"And you have the gall to leave before I've been given an opportunity to ask you a few questions, let alone defend myself?" She shook her head in pain. "Who are you? Once upon a time I thought I knew you."

"Touché," his voice rasped.

Aghast at his bitter response, an involuntary shudder racked Janet's body. His adversarial stance in front of her bespoke the enormity of the damage done by lies that had been passed off as truth.

"Ten years ago, you acted as judge, jury and executioner of our relationship. Just now, you did the same thing again, only you attacked me personally. For the sake of any feelings you once claimed to have for me, won't you at least do the honorable thing and give me equal time?" With the back of her hands, she wiped the tears off her cheeks. "You've leveled some pretty serious, even libelous indictments against me, you know."

He shifted his weight. "Is that a veiled threat? If I don't give you your day in court, can I expect you to haul me in under subpoena?" he inquired mildly.

With that question, something snapped inside Janet.

"There's no appealing to your better nature, is there? Evidently you lost it a long time ago." She opened the door for him, then walked swiftly to her desk. "Sandy? Tell Mr. Booth he can come back now."

"Janet..." She heard her name called as if it had come from some deep underground cavern.

"Don't worry," she assured him. "There'll be no subpoena."

He remained standing in place with his legs slightly apart, rubbing the back of his neck. "I shouldn't have said that. I had no right. What time will you be free later?"

She couldn't take this emotional roller-coaster ride any longer. "I have other plans."

"Change them."

"I can't. When I leave work, I'm expected at the homeless shelter."

There was a pregnant pause. "I thought you wanted to talk."

"I thought so, too, but I've changed my mind. Let's pretend you never came to my office. That way, you won't have to explain any of this to your wife. When you leave, it will be as if neither of us ever existed for the other. Goodbye, Wade."

At seven in the evening, a block-long line of people stood waiting for a meal outside the Salvation Army soup kitchen. If Wade recalled correctly, the downtown Salt Lake homeless shelter had to be close by.

He didn't know if it was the first excuse Janet had thrown at him to avoid another meeting. Yet helping the homeless sounded exactly like something she would do.

The one thing he could never accuse her of was a disregard of people in less fortunate circumstances than herself. She'd always championed the underdog, no matter the situation. It was little wonder she'd chosen to become a bankruptcy attorney.

Throughout their courtship, her guilt over having been born to money made her worry more than most people about the plight of the poor. Wade would laughingly tease her when she waxed too philosophical about a problem she couldn't fix. It was the only time she would get upset with him.

Hot color would fill her cheeks. Her eyes would turn an inky blue and her breasts would heave with emotion. "Someone *has* to care, Wade!"

"I know, sweetheart. But not tonight." Hungry for her mouth, he would possess it until she gave him back kiss for kiss, garnering all that exciting passion for himself.

She'd looked exactly like that earlier today when she'd stood in front of the door in an effort to bar him from leaving her office. Intense and passionate. It took him back to those halcyon days before his world had exploded into so many little bits he'd never been able to put it together again.

He drove his rental car around the corner until he spotted the sign he'd been looking for. Various automobiles were parked at curbside as well as in the lot adjacent to the building, but he didn't see any luxury foreign models she might own.

Aside from the fact that she'd always been a wealthy woman in her own right, being a member of the kind of prestigious law firm she'd joined guaranteed she could buy any make of car she wanted. But that wasn't her style, at least not the Janet he once knew.

He found a parking spot, then levered himself from the car and followed a couple of teenagers inside the entrance. The last-minute decision to change into jeans and T-shirt had been the right one.

A lot of adults were milling about. He spotted a middle-aged man at the front desk and approached him.

"I'm looking for Janet Larson. I understand she helps out here."

The other man smiled. "She's one of our mainstays. Follow that hallway to the end and take the stairs. You'll find her in the basement somewhere with the little kids."

She hadn't lied to him.

Suitably chastened, he began his search for her. With each stride he felt his heartbeat quicken, just like the old days when he had anticipated being with her after separation. The hardest thing about their relationship had been the times they were forced to spend apart.

Both of them had hated saying good-night. Finally he would relinquish her mouth before taking off for the apartment or the fraternity house. But she inevitably had called him back, breathless for one more kiss, which had turned into another until they lost count.

Lord, that was like a time out of time. There'd been many moments since then when he'd wondered if it had all been part of some fantastic dream. The man he'd become could no longer relate....

The lower floor of the shelter had been turned into a play center for the children. Maybe thirty of them, their ages ranging from four to eight, were busy doing various activities around the big room. Some young people who looked to be college-aged, appeared to be working with them in groups, either watching a cartoon, coloring or playing with toys.

As his gaze surveyed the scene, he caught sight of Janet sitting on the floor in the far corner of the room surrounded by a group of the youngest children. She held one of them on her lap while she read them a story.

Inexpressibly moved by the sight, he started toward her. Tonight she'd drawn her glossy black hair into a ponytail. Janet would always look elegant, even if she wore sackcloth and ashes. But dressed in a T-shirt and Levi's, she didn't appear much older than the other helpers in the room.

No one would guess she was the brilliant, successful attorney dressed to kill he'd confronted earlier today. She was so involved in telling the story, she hadn't spotted him yet.

"'When morning came, she lifted her head and her tear-drenched eyes saw the sweetest, most adorable little house. The forest creatures urged her forward.

"'"Hello? Is anyone inside?" she called out. No one answered, so she opened the door. And there before her stood a little wooden table with seven little chairs. Upstairs she counted seven little beds.

"'"Goodness," she cried. "This house must belong to seven little children who don't have a mother.

Their beds aren't made, and the dishes still need to be washed. Maybe if I make everything tidy and fix a good meal, they'll let me stay with them.''''"

A lump lodged in Wade's throat while he watched the way the children gazed at her in awe as she made the famous story come alive for them.

Why not? As he continued to look at Janet, he realized her coloring matched the description from the Brothers Grimm collection of fairy tales. "Lips as red as blood, skin as white as snow, and hair as black as ebony."

The more he thought about it, the more he understood why the words of the magic mirror had sent the wicked queen into a rage. No other woman could possibly compete against the maiden's rare beauty, not if she looked like Janet.

In the process of getting down on his haunches to listen, he drew her attention and heard a gasp. Her brilliant blue eyes stared at him as if she couldn't believe what she was seeing.

"Keep on reading, Snow White," he murmured. "You've got seven little dwarfs waiting on your every word."

After a prolonged silence, she finished the classic tale. Several times her voice faltered. He had no right to hope that it was his nearness that affected her, yet part of him relished the idea.

Heaven knew he'd already fallen under her spell once more. He'd sensed in his gut this would happen if he came after her tonight. But the memory of her tear-stained face, the pain in her voice before he'd left her office, had slipped past his defenses.

There was nothing she could say that would change

the agony of the past, but if he wanted closure on that period of his life, he knew he had to walk through the fire one more time.

"Come on, children. Enough stories for you. It's time for bed. Let's go upstairs and find your parents."

"Will you be here tomorrow night?" one of the boys in the circle asked.

"Not tomorrow night, but the next."

By now, the little girl on her lap had fallen asleep against her shoulder. Without asking permission, Wade reached for her so Janet could take care of the others. Together they started across the room with her holding on to the hands of two of the children.

Halfway up the stairs, a staggering pain almost incapacitated him. He realized that if things had turned out differently, they could be tucking their own children into bed before retiring to their bedroom for a night of lovemaking.

Wade had been robbed of that pleasure.

As pictures of her with Ty flashed into his mind, his world turned black once more.

She cast him a guarded glance. "I'll have to stay here in the lounge until their parents claim them. If you came to accuse me of more crimes, you might have to wait a few minutes."

"I'm not going anyplace," he ground out. "At least, not tonight."

Her face blanched before she urged the children to sit down.

"Janet?" The man Wade had seen at the desk earlier walked over to them. "If you want to leave, I'll take care of the kids." He reached for the little girl Wade had been holding against his shoulder. "Thanks for helping."

Janet seemed to hesitate, then thought better of it. "Any time. You know that. Good night, John."

"Good night."

Without looking at Wade, she walked out of the lounge and down the hall toward the entrance. A lot of the homeless were congregated in front of the shelter. Undoubtedly they were thankful for the warm night.

She greeted a considerable number of people who addressed her by her first name, proof that she was no stranger to the group. Many male eyes followed her progress. There seemed to be more men than women standing around on the grounds.

Wade didn't know another female who would come down here at night alone and unescorted. He didn't like it, but he had no right to voice an opinion.

"Where are you parked?"

"In the lot."

"Are you hungry?"

"No." She continued walking.

"I'm staying at the Temple View Hotel. Meet me in the bar for a drink in ten minutes."

"That might not be a good idea." Her voice shook. "I wouldn't want people to hear us."

Neither would he, not when his mood was this primitive. He'd only suggested it to test the waters. "Let's take a drive."

He felt her pause mid stride. "All right. I'll follow you to the hotel so you can drop off your car. We'll go in mine from there."

During the year and a half they'd dated, Wade hadn't

ridden in her family's BMW more than three or four times altogether. It was a matter of pride with him. As often as possible, he'd borrowed his dad's car.

Later, when his father returned to Colorado, Wade had bought a cheap secondhand car. Unfortunately it had given him a lot of trouble and had finally died. But at least throughout the greater part of their relationship, *he* had been the one to provide transportation.

Tonight he didn't give a damn how they arranged things. This final confrontation had been predestined since their accidental meeting in Mr. Loomis's office.

After accompanying her across the lot to an older model, blue convertible with the top down, he got behind the wheel of his rental car and headed for the hotel less than a mile away.

Taking advantage of the valet parking, he emerged from the hotel lobby after a few minutes and levered himself into her car. He didn't say anything until they merged with the traffic.

"As I recall, you always wanted a convertible. I had no idea one like this was still around."

"I bought it from a car collector."

"It looks in mint condition."

"Looks can be deceiving."

Her comment didn't escape him as she drove toward the state capital on the hill overlooking the city.

"No ride up one of the canyons?" They'd both loved the mountains.

"Not tonight. I prefer some place totally private where I know we won't be disturbed."

The capital grounds were one of the most public

places he could think of. But there was no second-guessing her.

"You've done well for yourself, Janet. A law degree from Stanford. I'm impressed."

"Not as impressed as I am that Rocky Mountain Enterprises is yours."

"You mean you're shocked that the poor boy actually made good?"

"I didn't say that!" she defended. "You *know* that wasn't what I meant!" Color stained her cheeks. "I think maybe it would be better if I took you back to the hotel."

She started to turn the wheel, but he reached out to hold it steady. "We've come this far," he muttered. "Let's finish it."

His goading had found its mark. He would have apologized, but he'd inadvertently brushed her hand. The touch of her skin sent a remembered current of electricity through his body, driving every thought out of his mind. All he craved was to feel her in his arms again.

Lord. Ten years, separation had only rekindled his passion. If it was possible, he wanted her more than ever. No longer a twenty-year-old boy, he was a man now, hot with a man's desire.

Fighting ambivalent emotions of bitterness and need, he forced himself to look away from her. To his surprise, she drove past the capitol to a section of luxury homes built above the city.

"You live up here?"

"No," she said quietly. "Annabelle does."

Annabelle. He smiled in fond remembrance of Janet's

best friend from the past. "Are you two still thick as thieves?"

"She's married now, but we're still close. While you were returning your car, I phoned her and got permission to use their backyard to talk."

Obviously Janet didn't trust them to be anywhere near other people.

Her instincts were right on. Since their chance meeting at Loomis's office, Wade had been out of control and she knew it. So much for the civilized discussion he'd had in mind. *Hell.*

CHAPTER THREE

JANET stood a few feet away from Wade. She watched
him as he walked to the edge of the velvety green lawn
and looked out at the spectacular view of the city whose
lights sprawled in all directions a thousand feet below
them.

The warm, fragrant night affected her senses until she
felt the throb of longing through her whole body, even
to her palms. Fresh guilt tormented her because she
couldn't suppress these feelings for him when she knew
he was a married man.

"From this vantage point, it feels like I'm in the cock-
pit of an airplane flying into Salt Lake at a low angle."

"It always takes my breath away," she admitted, but
in truth *he* was the one who by his mere presence had
turned her into a trembling supplicant.

Suddenly he wheeled around. She wasn't prepared for
the mood swing that caused his hands to curl into fists,
his features to look chiseled. Pained silvery eyes narrowed on her upturned features.

"What happened, Janet?" he murmured in a gravelly
tone. "When did you start to lose interest in me? In us?"

"Never!" her cry rang out in the darkness. Her heart
was hammering so hard she felt sick. "How could you
even ask me a question like that when you know how
crazy in love I was with you? You were my life, Wade!"
Her voice shook. "You *have* to know it!"

44

She heard a sharp intake of breath. "Then why did you make love with Ty Clark while I was in Denver talking to my folks about our wedding plans?"

Janet shook her head so hard the elastic snapped, sending the silky black hair flying around her face. "I've never made love with Ty or any man. Not even you," she replied in a throbbing voice.

Wade's complexion paled beneath the stars.

"The only man I ever wanted was you," she cried in renewed pain. "Who told you that lie?" she demanded furiously.

New lines of agony bracketed his mouth. "Who else but Ty himself."

"That's impossible! Ty and I have been friends since we were little kids. You and I were engaged to be married. He would never make up a story as cruel and wicked as that."

Wade's features looked carved out of rock. "Are you accusing me of lying?"

The tension between them could have lit up another city. Hot tears trickled down her cheeks.

"I'm not accusing you of anything. Just give me a minute to try and make sense of this. I feel like I'm in a nightmare."

"Tell me about it." The words sounded more like a snarl.

"He honestly told you we made love?" she cried again in disbelief. "When did he say this? I want to hear all of it, Wade! The exact words. Don't leave anything out."

"You're sure?" his voice mocked.

Even now, he wasn't convinced.

Dear God.

"If you don't believe me, then we'll drive over to Ty's house tonight. In front of you, I'll make him tell me word for word what he said to you."

After she'd thrown out the challenge, Wade's expression underwent a subtle change. He looked haunted.

"When I went to Denver that weekend to discuss our wedding plans with the folks, I found I didn't want to be away from you that long, so I flew home the next afternoon to surprise you. To my chagrin, I couldn't find you anywhere.

"Around eight that evening, a couple of the guys at the fraternity house suggested that maybe you were with Ty because they'd seen you with him the day before. I didn't know what in the hell that was supposed to mean.

"Finally Ty came over to the house like he usually did at night. I was waiting for him on the front porch and confronted him. He acted evasively, and seemed to enjoy it. I wouldn't let it alone. He finally agreed to tell me what was going on.

"We walked across the street to the grounds of the observatory where we could talk in private. That's when all hell broke loose."

Janet moved closer to him. "What did he say?"

Wade put his hands in the pockets of his jeans. "'I hate to have to be the one who tells you the truth, dude, but the fact is, Janet couldn't be in love with you. Around noon she called my house and asked if she could see me. She said she didn't want me to tell anyone else about it.

"'Janet and I have been friends since grade school. Naturally I said sure because I figured the two of you had had a fight and she needed a shoulder to cry on while you were out of town. She came by my house in her car and we drove up the canyon.

"'She was quiet on the way up. Suddenly she pulled into a vacant camping area and broke down crying about how she was feeling rushed into marriage. She talked a lot about her fears, that one day you might have the same problem with alcohol as your dad and not be able to hold down a good job.

"'I tried to comfort her, but she kept going on about how she wished your family had some money and measured up to one like mine. Pretty soon she was all over me.

"'One thing led to another, and hell, Wade, she knows I've always been attracted to her. That's the reason I didn't go away to college. What's a guy to do when a girl like Janet comes on to you? I mean she's a beautiful girl, and you do reach a point of no return. You know what I'm saying?

"'I never intended for you to learn about this until she told you. But it isn't as if you're formally engaged with a diamond.

"'Unfortunately a couple of the guys saw Janet and me together later when we stopped at the Canyon Inn for a burger. Naturally I didn't say a word about what happened, but I guess they just jumped to conclusions.'"

Until the shock waves subsided, Janet had buried her face in her hands. Finally she lifted her head, uncaring that he could see the tears dripping off her chin.

"In the beginning, I suspected Ty was jealous of you," she began, "but I thought he'd outgrown it by college. Who would have dreamed it was a pathological jealousy? I had no idea he was capable of doing anything as destructive as trampling on your vulnerability, let alone telling you such monstrous lies.''

The stillness emanating from Wade chilled her.

''They weren't all lies, Janet. How do you explain the guys telling me they saw you and Ty at the Canyon Inn that day?'' came his tortured whisper.

She stared into his eyes. ''That part is true. I called Ty and asked him to drive up the canyon with me. If you recall, you told me to pick the place for our reception and it would be fine with you.''

''I remember. I was fairly certain your parents would want to throw a big posh affair at the country club. Since you were their only child, I figured it would make them happy.''

Janet shook her head. ''Mom and Dad planned their own wedding. They said you and I should do the same. Whatever we wanted was fine with them.''

''So you went to the Canyon Inn?''

''Yes. I couldn't wait to surprise you with the news that we could have our wedding reception there, but first I had to make certain it was available for the date we'd picked.

''I purposely asked Ty along because he was president of your freshmen group of guys who joined the fraternity in the fall of that year. He would be the one in charge of getting the guys together to serenade us at our reception. I needed to be certain there weren't any other fraternity activities going on that night.''

Wade's jaw hardened. ''If you're telling the truth,

then your request would have been like throwing acid in Ty's face.''

''But at the time I didn't know that,'' she reminded him in a quiet voice. ''In my mind, it was important that he know what a thrill it would be for your family, not only to hear the guys sing, but to meet your friends, especially the ones who'd joined the fraternity when you did and lived at the house with you.''

''Go on,'' he muttered.

''It's hard when I know you're remembering Ty's lies.''

''I'm listening, Janet.''

She sucked in her breath. ''All right. The manager of the Canyon Inn was glad Ty had come with me since she said all those details should be worked out ahead of time. She walked us through the place and instructed Ty where the guys should sing. I arranged for a piano and a mike. She gave me some sample menus to look over with you.

''As a thank-you for his help, I bought Ty dinner. He promised he would work everything out with the president of the upper classmen of the fraternity so that everyone would be there and you wouldn't know anything about it until the night of our reception.''

He eyed her shrewdly. ''That's when a couple of the guys saw you?''

''Yes. I asked Ty not to tell them the reason why we were there. Until I talked to you about having our reception at the inn, I didn't want him saying a word to anybody.

''After I dropped him off at his house, I went to mine,

then flew down to Los Angeles with Mom. We spent the next day with my aunt looking for my wedding dress. I found the one I wanted and we flew back late Saturday night.''

"That's the reason I couldn't find you, because you were in Los Angeles?" he challenged grimly.

"Yes! You can call my aunt if you want. She'll verify it. I had no idea you'd come home from Denver a day early to surprise me. I—I never suspected there was a Mr. Hyde lurking inside Ty. He deliberately destroyed our lives!"

Janet didn't know what kind of reaction to expect out of Wade, but it wasn't his unnatural silence as he continued to scrutinize her through veiled eyes.

Aghast, she cried, "You don't believe me!"

"Frankly I don't know what to think. Ty was as earnest as you are. Even if everything you told me is true, you two still had time to be alone together."

A groan escaped her. "In other words, this comes down to circumstantial evidence. His testimony against mine." She shook her head in agony. "Was our whole relationship a lie to you?" she shouted, but she was in too much pain to care. "Where was the trust, Wade? That you could believe anything he'd said until you came to me for an explanation means our marriage would never have stood the test of time anyway. Without total faith in each other, it wouldn't have worked."

How could I have been so wrong about anyone?

She knew she was going to be ill. "I don't want to talk anymore. I don't know who you are. Obviously I never did. The sight of you sickens me." She reached in her purse and threw the keys on the ground at his feet. "You can drive my car back to the hotel and leave the keys at the front desk. I'll pick it up later. I only pray to God I never have to see you again in my lifetime."

Turning on her heel, she fled toward the house. He called her name, but she kept on running. There was footfall behind her before he grabbed her by the arms.

"Let me go!" she screamed hysterically, then went limp as she proceeded to be sick right in front of him.

The back lights went on. Suddenly Rand and Annabelle appeared on the patio.

"Janet? What's wrong?" Annie rushed over to her.

"She's sick to her stomach," Wade answered for her while he steadied her in his powerful arms.

"Tell him to go away, Annie," Janet begged her friend. "Please…"

"Rand darling? Would you mind running Wade back to his hotel while I take care of Janet?"

"Of course not. Come through here to reach the garage, Wade."

If anything, Wade's hands tightened on her arms for a brief moment before she felt him relinquish his hold of her.

"I'll call you tomorrow," he vowed before reluctantly following Rand across the patio, but Janet was too busy being sick again to tell him it would be a wasted effort. Tonight the past had been buried forever.

"What hotel are you staying at?"

"The Temple View."

Rand reversed the Mercedes out of the driveway past Janet's car, and they were off.

"I'm going to be up front with you right now, Wade. I love Janet like a sister. She's been through too much where you're concerned to go through any more."

Wade didn't need Annabelle's husband to warn him off. Watching Janet be sick—knowing he was the one responsible—had made him so ill he felt like he'd been kicked repeatedly in the gut.

"I gather you've never made such an error in judgment that it blew up in your face and shattered every dream."

"Want to make a bet?"

"With Annie, I mean."

"Who else? After we got engaged, I demanded she leave the police force and be a stay-at-home wife. She threw the ring at me and went back to Salt Lake. It took me a whole year to figure out what a complete jerk I was. Life had no meaning without her. That's when I went after her and ended up living here."

"But you only made a near-fatal mistake with her one time. I did it again tonight. Janet's not going to give me another chance to get near her."

"Nope."

That one word pounded him further down the sink-hole. "No matter what happened between us, I can't let her go again, Rand. She's my life!"

"Even if you feel that way, you don't have the right to do anything about it. Not with a wedding band on your finger."

"I wear it to keep things less complicated. The truth is, I've been divorced for three years."

There was a prolonged silence. "Does Janet know you're free?"

"No."

Rand flashed him an accusing glance. "What in the hell are you trying to do to her?"

"I presumed Janet had a husband. It was easier facing her with it on. My ex-wife was right. When we married, there were three of us. Claire, myself and Janet. Claire finally got tired of the company and moved on."

"*Good Lord.* You remind me so much of myself a few years ago it's like déjà vu."

Wade felt a grudging respect for Rand Dunbarton. "Have you got any advice?"

"Annabelle tells me you and Janet were soul mates from the first day you met in high school. It might help if you told me what made you break your engagement to her."

Wade sucked in his breath. "That could take a while."

"I don't have anywhere else to go. Right now, it's probably better that Janet spend some time alone with Annabelle. As I understand it, my wife helped her pick up the pieces ten years ago when you didn't come back to Salt Lake."

It sounded so strange to hear Rand talk about picking up the pieces. All these years Wade had believed Janet and Ty must have gotten married. They were the perfect society couple. Both families had money. Even the guys on the football team had decreed marriage was their destiny. But putting those assumptions aside, Ty had been so damn convincing.

Janet just told you it was all lies. That fateful day, she had been up the canyon planning the kind of wedding reception you wanted. She was trying to do something to make you happy. When you couldn't find her, it was because she'd gone to California to buy the perfect wedding dress so she would look beautiful for you.

It was all for you, and you pushed her away. You wouldn't even let her come to Denver to talk to you.

If her truth *was* the truth—and he was beginning to believe it was—then he'd allowed his pain to take away ten years of rapture and fulfillment they could never have back.

Tears flooded his eyes before his fists turned into balls against his thighs.

Janet wiped her tears, hugged Annabelle and said good-night. It was after eleven. Rand would be home soon. She didn't want to be there when he returned. No postmortems.

She couldn't handle the fact that Ty Clark was capable of such shocking, cold-blooded treachery and betrayal when she'd thought he was a good friend. She never wanted to see him or hear his name again in her lifetime.

As for Wade, after listening to his explanation, it didn't seem possible that he hadn't believed in their love enough to give them a chance to work things out. She'd spent ten years grieving for a love he didn't even try to fight for.

It was a worse betrayal than anything Ty had done to them because Wade knew better. After a year and a half of constant togetherness, he *knew* he was her whole life, yet he hadn't come to her when their very existence as an engaged couple hung in the balance.

She was through.

No more thinking about the past. Not ever!

On the drive back to her condo in a high-rise building at the mouth of Emigration Canyon, she made up her mind to return Dave Jessop's phone call. Though he'd attended her high school, they hadn't really known each other. Since graduation, he'd been at college back east and had ended up at Harvard Business School.

A few weeks ago, she'd bumped into him at a downtown restaurant at lunchtime. During the course of their conversation, she'd learned the good-looking blond bachelor had returned home as the new vice president of the Maxfield department stores, a Western state's chain whose headquarters were in Salt Lake.

It had been interesting to talk about old times and mutual acquaintances—that is, until he mentioned Wade's name. To his credit, Dave didn't pry, but when he found out she was still single, he said he would call her for a date.

There could be no better time than right now to get to know him better. If she let memories of Wade prevent her from exploring what might be between her and the men who were seeking a relationship with her, then her depression would grow much worse. Inevitably she'd be forced to seek the professional counseling her mother had suggested.

What was that awful cliché? *Tomorrow is the first day of the rest of your life.*

Determined to make a new one for herself no matter that she was dying inside, she parked the car in her stall on the third level of the condo complex, then walked to the door, which could only be accessed with a remote she carried on her key ring.

Halfway over the threshold, she sensed someone directly behind her. Terror seized her heart because she hadn't seen a soul coming in or out of the building. Fearing an attack or something worse, she felt for the special pepper-spray device Annabelle had given her to put on her key ring, wheeled around and started spraying.

"Wade!" she cried out in shock when she realized he was the one groaning in pain. His hands had gone to his eyes.

Annabelle had assured Janet the spray was not permanently harmful, but it would cause intense stinging and momentarily distract a would-be assailant.

Remorse followed on the heels of her fear. "I'm so sorry, Wade." Her voice shook. "I didn't know it was you. I—I thought—"

"I know what you thought," he cut in. "You did exactly the right thing," he muttered, weaving a little on his feet.

Had the spray made him unsteady, as well?

"It was too easy to sneak up on you out here. Lord—that stuff really works! It feels like acid eating my eyes."

Fresh guilt attacked her. "Come in the condo. You need to wash them with water."

"I'm afraid you're going to have to lead me," he confessed. "I can't see where in the hell I'm going. I had a vile headache earlier and took a strong painkiller. I'm afraid the reaction has caught up with me."

Forgetting everything but the need to put him out of

his misery as soon as possible, she reached for his arm and guided him down the hall to the second door on the left. His body fell heavily against her several times.

He'd always been strong, but ten years had made his physique even more powerful. Their hips brushed as they walked, sending little arrows of awareness through her body. Despite his condition, she couldn't help but be affected by his nearness. The scent of the shampoo he used in the shower was the same as before, taking her back in time.

Now that she knew it was Wade, she was thankful no one had been around to see what she'd done to him. Hurriedly unlocking the front door, she helped him inside her traditionally furnished condo and rushed him through the hallway to the kitchen.

"Here." She turned on the faucet, regulating the water to the right temperature. "Just keep washing your eyes until the stinging stops. Maybe I should call a doctor for you."

"You don't need to do that," he said after several minutes of irrigating them. "Already I'm starting to feel some relief." His low, reassuring voice helped dissipate some of her anxiety for his welfare.

"I should never have done that without looking to see who it was first."

"*Thank God* you followed your instincts and didn't hesitate. If I had been a rapist, you'd have been dragged off somewhere by now." She shuddered at the thought. "Every woman should have such a deterrent handy."

"That's what Annabelle says," she concurred in a wobbling voice. "She gave it to me for Christmas years ago, but I've never had a reason to use it until—"

"Until I scared the hell out of you!" he cut in with self-deprecation. "Annabelle always was ahead of her time, but I do believe she met her match in Rand. He's a good man."

Janet swallowed hard. "He is. *The best*."

"I agree. He took pity on a man desperate enough to do anything to finish talking to you. Don't hate him too much for giving me your address. I told him I'd be in worse condition than you if I were prevented from seeing you tonight. You and I haven't begun to discuss what needs discussing."

His physical condition was making him act without inhibition. *This was no time for the kind of talk he had in mind*, her heart cried out. But until she knew his eyes would be all right, she didn't have the temerity to demand that he leave the condo.

Wade had always been tough whether it be at sports or anything else. The night he'd gone to the hospital with appendicitis, no one could have guessed at the kind of pain he was in because he always hid it so well.

Knowing this was his nature, she didn't buy his denial about the seriousness of his eye injury and would insist her doctor have a look at him first thing in the morning.

He finally raised his head. Water dripped off the smoothly shaven jaw she'd kissed probably thousands of times. "I think that ought to do it."

She handed him a clean dish towel from the drawer so he could wipe away the moisture.

"Look at me, Wade."

Damn. Why did her voice always tremble?

Still a bit unsteady on his feet, he slowly turned until he was facing her. Searching his eyes, she couldn't find anything outward to alarm her, but that didn't necessarily mean he was free of pain.

"Can you see me clearly?"

In her anxiety, she hadn't realized how close they were standing together. The body heat being generated between them felt like a fire being whipped up in the wind. Only breathtaking inches separated them.

"As I told you earlier tonight, you look like the painting out of everyone's favorite fairy tale."

How much of the painkiller was talking?

Her knees shook. "Don't lie to me. I have to know you're all right."

"What will it take to convince you?"

"I—I don't know. It's just that I feel so horrible for what I did to you."

She felt his hands lift to her shoulders and begin to knead them through the thin material of her T-shirt. Her body trembled. He shouldn't be here. And certainly not touching her like this. He belonged to someone else....

"I did something much, much worse to you tonight" came the tortured whisper. In a lightning change, she saw a mask slip down over his rugged features, hardening them. "I chose not to believe you."

His fingers bit into her skin, but she was positive it was unconscious on his part.

"Don't you see?" He shook her. "I *had* to believe you lied to me." She felt the shudders that racked his body. "Part of me still wants to believe you betrayed me." A cord stood out in his neck, evidence of his tension. "Otherwise how else could I go on living with the knowledge that *I'm* the one who destroyed our love? Not you."

His question reverberated throughout the condo, laying the wound wide open so that she was bleeding profusely once more.

In abject despair, she shook her head and backed away, forcing him to relinquish his hold of her. A cold chill entered her body where his hands had been. But she didn't have the right to want them there. Another woman wore his wedding ring.

"None of it matters anymore," she forced herself to say. "You lost trust in me ten years ago, and now it's too late. We can't go back and repair the damage. If you've really recovered from the spray, I'd like you to leave."

His powerful frame tautened. "I have no intention of going anywhere."

Grabbing the nearest chair back, she beseeched him with her eyes. "You've said what you came to say. Isn't that enough? Now go. Please—"

"Why?" He persisted. "I know you don't want me to. We have ten years of catching up to do."

"That's where you're wrong." She drew in a deep breath, realizing it was up to her to keep things from getting out of hand. "Wherever the fault really lies, our broken engagement is a thing of the past. You married someone else.

"If your wife knows about our history, then she'll understand why we needed this time for closure. But she won't understand anything else and shouldn't have to. Maybe infidelity is the only subject you and I never discussed during our relationship. In case you don't know, I put it on a par with murder. Go home to her, Wade."

There was a long silence. "I can't."

She frowned. "What do you mean?"

"Claire divorced me three years ago. Now she's happily married to someone else."

Janet had lived through several shocks tonight, but this one made her heart skip around like a firework gone berserk.

"You haven't taken off your wedding ring. Are you still so in love with your ex-wife you're in denial?"

He rubbed the back of his neck absently. "On the contrary. For the two years we were married, she accused me of never being in love with her."

Coming on the tail of the other, this revelation knocked Janet sideways.

"In my gut I knew she was right," he continued, "so I decided it might make my future safer and less complicated all the way around if I kept the ring on. It never occurred to me I would run into you in Loomis's office."

"Or you would have removed it?" she threw out the question. "Is that what you're saying?" She shook her head. "Why weren't you honest with me when you came to my office?"

The air was heavy with tension. "As I told you earlier, I assumed you and Ty had married. I hid behind my former marriage because my pride couldn't handle either of you knowing that it had failed."

She still didn't understand. "A marriage that doesn't work must be very sad, but it isn't something to be ashamed of, surely."

His eyes narrowed. "You've missed my point."

"Just say what you have to say!" she cried out in pain and frustration.

"My marriage didn't stand a chance because I had never fallen out of love with *you*."

Janet gasped at the admission.

"Claire's miscarriage was like an omen. To my relief, we divorced some time later. She's a wonderful person who deserved to meet someone who would truly love her. That day finally came for her.

"As for me, when I saw you again—" there was a slight pause "—I wanted you to think I was as happy with my wife as I presumed you to be with Ty. I would've done anything to pretend I hadn't suffered permanent damage over your betrayal.

"You have to understand something. When we were in high school, you convinced me that my moneyless background didn't matter. You never judged my father. You didn't care that I didn't have a car, let alone an expensive one. Your love made me feel safe and secure.

"There were guys on the football team who told me it wouldn't last. They said the Janet Larsons of this world always reverted to type in the end."

She winced inwardly because she knew selfish, insecure people talked like that, thought like that.

"When I was asked to join the fraternity, there were other guys who said the only reason I got in was because I was dating Janet Larson. If I'd been dating anyone else, it would never have happened."

Every awful thing she was hearing now caused her heart to wrench a little more.

He smiled, but it didn't reach his haunted gray eyes. "I refused to believe them, let alone listen. You would've had to live in my shoes all these years to understand the amount of pleasure it gave me when Loomis told you I was the owner of Rocky Mountain Enterprises. I knew you would tell your husband. Proving you both wrong came as a bittersweet moment for me. I received a perverse thrill when you ran out on your client. Checkmate at last.''

His mouth tightened into a thin line. ''But the second you disappeared from his office, the victory grew hollow. Pandora's box had been opened and I found myself at your office determined to make you pay.''

Janet stood there in mute shock. She could tell Wade was living the horrifying past all over again. His mind wouldn't let go of the lies, but she couldn't blame him. Not after the damage Ty had done.

She thought she'd known all there was to know about Wade. But she'd had no conception of how fragile he'd really been during the period of his parents' divorce. His tough facade had hidden a multitude of insecurities she was only beginning to understand.

Her father had called Wade a coward for not being able to face Janet with the truth. But he hadn't known the facts behind Wade's decision to break up with her. No one knew the truth.

Except Ty himself.

Just now, Wade had allowed her to break through his defenses for a few seconds. It was long enough to understand why his psyche had been in so much pain he couldn't have faced her back then.

Ty had trampled all over their love with his lies. Too much damage had been inflicted. He'd led Wade to believe that he and Janet belonged to a secret club Wade could never join. Not only had he condemned Wade's father for his addiction problem, he'd told him his family would never be good enough, never measure up. He'd thrown it in Wade's face that Wade would never amount to anything in life, so why bother?

Knowing all this, she could never fault Wade for running away. No wonder he was incredulous when he'd charged into her office and found out she hadn't married Ty after all. She didn't fault Wade for anything. *Dear God.* She loved him! She'd never stopped!

"I have to give Ty full marks for his cunning," she conceded at last. "He combined just enough truth with his lies and crushing words to cripple you so completely you would go away and never come back. The worst of it is, after he accomplished his goal with you, he pretended to be my friend and started manipulating *me*." Her voice was shaking.

"Go on."

"When you ended our engagement, I couldn't handle it and had to drop out of school for the rest of the semester."

Lines darkened Wade's face.

"Ty would call me every day, or come by the house to try to cheer me up. He saw, he *knew* how devastated I was, yet he told me I was better off without you, that you had never really fitted in my world, and now you had shown your true colors."

"The bastard honestly said that?" Wade hissed.

"Yes. His words left me more shattered than ever. I lost twenty pounds right away. My parents made me see a doctor. I was put on medication until I could pull out of the worst of my grief.

"Through all this, no one could have been kinder than Ty. But when I started to function again and could go back to class, he got upset because I didn't rely on him for everything. I told him I didn't want to presume on our friendship. That's when he told me he was in love with me and wanted to marry me. You can't imagine how stunned I was.

"He knew I'd always been so much in love with you I could never see anyone else. At that point, I told him how grateful I was for his friendship, but it was *you* I wanted, no one else.

"Of course he was hurt, but he seemed to handle it. Within six months, he found a local girl and married her. I never met her and wasn't invited to the wedding. According to rumor, it only lasted a year because he was unfaithful."

"Where is he now?"

Janet flinched from the fury in his tone.

"The last I heard, he worked for the Linford Mortuary."

"Mortuary?"

"Apparently he married a second time. Do you remember Cindy Linford?"

"No."

"She went to our high school, but she was a year younger than we were. Someone told me they had a baby five months later." Silence stretched between them. She could read Wade's mind. "If you're planning to pay him a visit in the near future, I'm going with you."

"Tonight can't be too soon for me. But you're staying here!" He started for the front door of her condo.

She ran after him. "Because you still don't trust me?" she cried out in fresh pain. He was in no shape to go anywhere.

He raked unsteady hands through his hair. His sharp intake of breath sounded like ripping silk. "Because I'm not sure I trust myself not to kill him! I don't want you around to see it."

"Don't say that, Wade. Don't even think it! He's not worth one more second of your thoughts."

His complexion looked gray around the mouth. "After what you've just told me, I'm convinced Ty's not only sick, he's evil. Give me one good reason why he should be allowed to draw another breath."

"Because you always were the better man, and he couldn't handle it. If you confront him in your rage, then he'll have the last laugh. Don't you see?"

"You have another plan in mind?"

He stared at her, wild-eyed. Maybe he'd breathed in some of the pepper spray and it had mixed with the painkiller to make him irrational.

"Yes," she lied because she didn't know how else to stop him. "Yes, I do. But it's late. I was sick earlier, and you're still recovering from my attack on you. We both need some sleep so we can think clearly." Her voice cracked. "Y-you can stay on my couch tonight. Tomorrow will be soon enough to talk."

He looked stunned. "After everything I've done, you mean you would allow me to sleep here?"

Oh, darling. You haven't done anything wrong. Don't you know that?

Faking brightness, she said, "Of course."

His mouth twisted in what looked like a grimace of self-denigration. "You always did champion anyone down on his luck. But I won't say no to your offer," he rasped. "To be honest, I don't think I could make it out to the car."

"Quick, Wade! Hold on to me before you fall down!"

She staggered under his weight. Somehow they made it to the living room before he collapsed on the couch. Once she'd helped him to stretch out, his eyes closed and he didn't change his position.

Satisfied he wouldn't be getting up again, she went to the linen closet for some bedding.

He never noticed when she came back and removed his socks and shoes. In case he hadn't lost complete consciousness yet, she refrained from kissing his mouth. But as she tucked the quilt around him and slipped the pillow beneath his head, he would never know the control it took not to ravish him.

CHAPTER FOUR

A NOISE followed by some muttered imprecation Janet couldn't quite make out reached her ears. Wade! Was he sick?

She'd stayed awake most of the night listening for him in case he needed her. But she must have finally fallen asleep. Now her clock radio showed five-thirty in the morning.

After leaping out of bed, she threw on her terry-cloth bathrobe and ran out of her room to find him. Hearing another oath coming from the kitchen, she darted toward it.

When she entered, she could barely make out Wade's silhouette in the darkness. She flipped on the switch. He jerked around in surprise, almost dropping the mug in his hand.

"Why didn't you turn on the light?" she cried in alarm. "Are your eyes still in pain?"

"No."

"How is your headache?"

"It's gone. I was trying to be quiet so you could sleep, but I bumped into a chair in the dark."

He looked like he could use more sleep, but thank heaven that wild look had gone.

In bare feet, with his dark hair attractively disheveled, his T-shirt half tucked in the jeans riding low on his lean hips, he reminded her of the old Wade. He ran a hand

68

over his mouth and jaw where she could see the shadow of his beard.

After all these years, she never dreamed the day would come when he would be standing in her small kitchen looking too wonderful for words. However, it appeared he didn't share her opinion as he expelled a sigh of pure self-disgust.

"I thought a cup of coffee would get me going. Forgive me for disturbing you."

"I was awake," she lied without compunction. "I'm usually up by now. Why don't you sit down and I'll fix some for both of us?"

He moved slowly before lowering himself into one of the chairs of the old oak dinette set she'd bought at a used-furniture store and refinished herself.

While she reached for the instant coffee, she felt his slumberous gaze wander up her bare legs, where the hems of her matching cream nightgown and robe fell to the knee. A wave of heat followed the progress of that slow perusal as it made its way up the rest of her body to her hair. Fortunately the glossy black mane swung about her face and shoulders, half-hiding her rosy profile from view.

"One mug of coffee coming up for one big, grumpy dwarf," she teased as she pulled it from the microwave and set it in front of him. He liked it black. Alongside it, she placed a bowl of sugar with a spoon. Wade's only flaw had been a horrible sweet tooth.

She thought he would've drunk some of it by the time she joined him at the table with her own cup. Instead, his intelligent eyes studied her through thick, dark-fringed lashes. There was this amazing intensity coming from the gray irises with their crystalline outer ring.

Feeling a little breathless from his scrutiny, she said, "Have your habits changed? If you want cream, I have some in the refrigerator."

His enigmatic gaze remained on her a minute longer before he put three teaspoons of sugar in the steaming hot liquid and proceeded to drink it in small quantities just like he used to do until it was gone.

When he'd finished, he set the mug down, never taking his eyes off her. "As you can see, I still like it black and sweet. I'm surprised you remembered."

"There are some things you never forget," she somehow choked out before she sipped her coffee. "Are you feeling a little better now?"

He rubbed the side of his face with his hand. "How bad was I last night?"

She moistened her lips nervously. "After I accidentally sprayed you, you were in a lot of pain."

"Did I pass out on you?"

She was thankful he didn't remember their conversation about Ty. "More or less."

He bit out a word not worth repeating before getting to his feet. "I apologize."

"There's no need." Her voice trembled. "Last night we were both under a lot of stress."

"But I had no right to stalk you and then end up sleeping on your couch because I took too much pain medication and couldn't leave on my own two feet. *Hell.*"

"Please don't be so hard on yourself, Wade. There were extenuating circumstances."

"That's the understatement of the decade," he muttered savagely. After a pregnant silence, he asked, "How soon do you need to be at your office?"

"Not for three hours. Enough time for you to shower while I fix you a good breakfast. You might even feel human by then."

"Meaning I was some kind of monster last night."

"No!"

"The hell I wasn't! I seem to remember the conversation centering on Ty and a mortuary. We decided to table the discussion until morning." He had a mind like a steel trap. No doubt by the time he was fully awake, he would remember everything.

"He's not worth talking about."

"That's what you said last night," he shot back at her.

"Wade?" She rose to her feet, her heart beating too fast. "His lies robbed us of years we might have had together. To allow him another second of our time would mean we haven't learned anything from the past."

Wade's face closed up. "I want to hear his confession."

She felt the stab of another dagger because he would never be satisfied until he'd wrung the words from Ty himself.

"If he's as twisted as I think he is, I don't imagine he's capable of one."

"I could force it."

"Probably. But the Wade I once knew didn't have a violent bone in his body."

That bleak look she hated entered his eyes. "I'm not

the same man. If you think I'm going to let this go, then you never knew me at all.''

''You made that clear last night.''

She took the mugs to the sink to rinse them, her mind deep in thought over an idea she'd been considering ever since she made him comfortable on her couch.

Before she retired to her room for the night, she'd listened to the messages on her answering machine. Dave Jessop had called again, wanting to know if she would like to go to their high school's ten year reunion with him next month.

She'd received a flyer in the mail about it last week, but as soon as she read it, she'd tossed it in the wastebasket. The pain of seeing old high school friends who would ask her questions about Wade didn't bear thinking about.

If Wade hadn't suddenly reappeared in her life, she would have carried through with her plan to return Dave's calls and tell him she'd love to go to a film or the symphony, or any other function with him as long as they stayed away from the reunion.

But seeing Wade again like this made the thought of being with any other man repugnant to her, even Dave whom she'd found more attractive than most of her dates. Tomorrow she would have to find a way to discourage him without offending him too much.

As for the reunion itself, she imagined most everyone of the old crowd would be there. Certainly those who still resided in Salt Lake, but especially Ty who, as past president of the school, would be expected to preside over the event.

"Wade?"

"I'm right here."

She darted him a surprised glance. He'd found a clean dish towel and had started drying the mugs. Their gazes locked.

"I—I think I know a way we can see Ty again without it being confrontational. It might even intimidate him enough that he'll give himself away."

His hands stilled for a moment. "How?"

Resting her hip against the counter, she told him about the reunion. "If you and I showed up for it together, he would realize that his machinations hadn't worked after all."

Wade's lips twisted unpleasantly. "Bad idea. I've been coming to Salt Lake for the past couple of years. Several of the people we went to school with now work for banks and realty companies where I do business. I never bothered to disabuse anyone of the fact that I'm no longer married.

"Showing up at the reunion with my old high school sweetheart when I'm supposed to have a perfectly good wife at home would cause more than a few tongues to wag."

Her gaze flicked to the gold band on his finger. She'd been trying hard not to think about his ex-wife. The idea of her being the recipient of Wade's love, of sharing two precious years of intimacy with him even if they had divorced, was another pain that refused to go away.

"I don't care what other people think."

"Neither do I," he bit out. "But I can guarantee Ty would be the first person in line to ask about Claire while he secretly gloated over his success in tearing you and me apart." He paused momentarily. "You wouldn't want to be around me when that happened," he whispered savagely.

His rage was back. She needed to say something quick to dilute it. With a daring she didn't know she possessed, she ventured, "What if we made an entrance together a-as man and wife?"

Dark brows met in a straight line of incredulity. "You mean I should let people know I'm divorced, and we would pretend we were married using this band to prove it?"

It was hard to swallow. "No. I mean you should wear the ring I picked out for you ten years ago."

The kitchen took on an unearthly silence. She thought his complexion had paled a few degrees.

"You still have it?" His eyes searched hers as if he would probe the secrets of her soul.

Janet could hardly breathe. "Yes."

He seemed to be in some kind of a stupor. Part of him still didn't believe her about anything. What would it take?

"Just a minute, Wade. I'll be right back."

She dashed out of the kitchen to the guest bedroom that served as a large storage room. Except for a desk with her computer and fax machine, there was no other furniture in it yet. In the closet lay the huge rectangular box that once stored her heavy, full-length cashmere coat. Rising on tiptoe, she tugged at the corners with her fingers to get it down.

"Allow me." Wade had followed her into the room. With matchless male grace, he extricated the box from the shelf. "Where would you like it?"

"Where would *you*?" she countered with another question. "Three-quarters of the things in there are yours."

His expression underwent another transformation. He reminded her of someone who had gone into shock.

She took the box from his hands and walked to the living room, where she rested it on the coffee table. With some difficulty, she removed the lid. "I haven't looked inside this for a long time," she quavered.

Wade's gaze fastened on the eight-by-ten, black-and-white glossy of the two of them dancing at the fraternity's winter fest formal. Next to it were their high school graduation pictures in color, along with their diplomas, tassels and the program of the exercises.

Like a person moving in slow motion, he approached the treasure trove of memories. She saw his hand shake as he opened the thick scrapbook and started turning page after page. Snaps in every shape and size of the two of them taken for the fun of it on picnics, hikes, water-skiing outings, at dances, parties, at the beach, in the mountains.

Twenty minutes must have passed before he reached for the Kansas City Royals baseball cap he'd always worn backward to games. Then came a medal on a chain he'd won for the fastest 440 yard dash. She watched the pile on the table spill onto the floor. There were all kinds of awards they'd both won for debate meets, sports, music, scholarship.

Next he drew out his old high school letter jacket. He'd made her wear it one night when it had gotten too cold on their bike ride. The jacket had ended up in her closet. She'd told Wade she wanted to keep it to show their children. He seemed to have approved of the idea because he ended up kissing her senseless that night.

Maybe he was remembering, which could explain why he stood there clutching the shoulders of the jacket in his hands. Finally he laid it on the couch and reached for the exquisite little painted enamel jewelry box from Germany he'd given her their first Christmas.

When the lid was opened, it played the love song Don José sang to *Carmen*, one of Janet's favorite operas. Wade had taken her to see it at the opera house. After he'd given her the Christmas present, he admitted he'd searched weeks to find the perfect tune. It was probably her most cherished possession. But after he'd broken off their engagement, she'd put it away, unable to bear hearing the music. It hurt too much.

Her breath caught as he lifted the lid and the beautiful love song filled her living room, taking her back in time. While it played, Wade found his fraternity pin, the one he'd given her the night he'd formally proposed to her. His fraternity ring lay next to it, the promise implicit that one day they would be married.

There was more....

As he opened the small black velvet ring box, her heart felt like it was going into fibrillation. Tucked inside was the inlaid black-and-gold wedding band she'd had custom made for him. It was unique, one of a kind and very masculine. Like Wade himself.

"There's an inscription," she offered quietly. "If you turn on the lamp, you'll be able to read it."

Like a sleepwalker, he moved toward one of her brass lamps with the pleated shades.

For the year and a half that they'd dated, she didn't

think a day had gone by that she hadn't whispered against his lips, "You're *my* man. Don't ever forget it." Those words were followed by a final kiss that went on and on.

It was one of those private little things between lovers that became a ritual. When the jeweler had asked her what she'd like engraved on the band, she didn't hesitate to tell him. The truth was, she couldn't wait for Wade to see it.

Little did she know the moment would have to be postponed ten years.

When Wade finally raised his head, his solemn expression was eloquent with meaning.

He liked it. She could tell he did.

"Why don't you try it on and see if it fits?"

At first she thought he would put it on the finger of his right hand. Instead, he removed the band Claire had given him and put it in his pocket.

The significant gesture caused her to tremble.

"Why don't you come over here and do the honors?" he whispered silkily.

With heart thudding, she got up from the Italian provincial chair with its jade moiré covering and approached him.

The ring sat in the palm of his left hand.

Gingerly she picked it up and turned his hand over. Then she slid it home without any trouble. How many times in her dreams had she imagined doing that at their wedding ceremony?

"I believe this is where I get to kiss my bride."

She never questioned what happened next. Her mouth rushed to meet his. Automatically her hands slid up his chest to encircle his neck, impatient to get as close to him as was humanly possible. It was like a miracle feeling the familiar, hard-muscled length of his body against hers again.

Exploding with needs that couldn't be satisfied fast enough, they kissed with primitive hunger. "Wade..." she gasped as they gave each other long kisses, short kisses. Breathless kisses that covered eyes, cheeks, throats, lashes, lips and mouths starving for each other.

She moaned in ecstasy as his hands moved over her back and hips, drawing her inexorably tighter against him until it felt like they had melded into one swaying entity of rapture.

"*Janet*," he groaned, "it's been too long. In another second, I'm going to devour you completely."

"I wish you would!" Janet's cry was embarrassingly uninhibited. But this was Wade in her arms, kissing and caressing her with a refined savagery more overwhelming than the passion they'd generated years ago. She couldn't deny him anything, otherwise she might just as well stop breathing.

"I want you so badly I'm shaking like a man with palsy," he admitted against her mouth. "But this is too easy, Janet. It feels too good. I don't have the right to do what I want to do to you. Not after everything that's happened."

His words signaled a death knell. She wouldn't let him do this. Not now! He was back in her life and she was going to fight for him with every weapon at her disposal.

"You've always had the right," she declared before pressing her mouth to his once more, refusing to let him move out of her arms. "I love you, Wade. I've always loved you. You're my man," she whispered into his neck. "Did you forget?" She kissed his jaw. "Because if you did, I'll help you remember. Give me your left hand, darling."

She relinquished her hold of him enough to clasp it between hers. After kissing each fingertip, she raised imploring blue eyes to his. "Last time you asked me the question. Now I'm going to ask you.

"Will you marry me, Wade? Will you be my husband? I don't care where we live or what we do as long as it's together from now on. I've existed during the past ten years, but you couldn't call it living. There's no life without you! The yawning emptiness has proved that.

"It doesn't matter about the past. It's behind us. But there's still a future out there. Our future. The one we talked about every day."

He sucked in his breath. "You think it's possible to put all the agony of the past behind us?" he grated.

"Yes!" she blurted. "Don't you?"

His eyes continued to penetrate hers, but they were full of doubts. "I'm not sure."

Because you still don't trust me?

She'd wanted his honesty, but it was so painful she could hardly bear it. Swallowing hard, she said, "Do you remember our last phone call?"

He nodded almost imperceptibly.

"Do you remember the last thing I said to you?"

Another silence. "At that low period in time, I was

in such a traumatic state, I had no idea what was real or imagined.''

"Then I'll refresh your memory. I told you that if the day ever came when you wanted to talk to me, I would be here waiting for you because there would never be another man for me. As you can see, I'm still here,'' she said, her voice shaky. "I'm still waiting.'' Her mother had been right about that after all. "You do love me, don't you?''

Another muttered imprecation passed his lips as he raked unsteady hands through his hair. "That's not the point, Janet.''

"Then what is?'' she persisted. He hadn't denied his love for her. That was all she needed to know before daring to suggest what she'd wanted with all her heart and soul from the first time she'd met him. "Would you like me to stay home and be your full-time wife?''

"You mean you would give up the lucrative law practice you've worked for all these years?'' he scathed as if the idea were ludicrous.

"I would do it in a heartbeat. I would do *anything* to be with you,'' she admitted tearfully.

"Maybe you would at that,'' he murmured cryptically.

Whatever he meant by those words, it couldn't be good. She groaned because the damage Ty had inflicted had gone so deep. But she refused to give up now.

"If I weren't working, we could build that dream home we used to talk about. Maybe we could find a piece of property somewhere in the mountains near Denver. It wouldn't have to be a long commute to your office. That way, we'd stay close to your family, as well.''

"No, Janet."

This implacable side of him staggered her.

"Because of Claire?" She'd been trying hard not to be jealous of the other woman who'd known him intimately. It hurt so much she needed to stop dwelling on it or she'd go mad.

"No," he said more quietly this time. "That wouldn't be a problem even if she still lived there. As it is, they moved to Grand Junction where her husband works."

"Then what you're trying to tell me is, you don't want to marry me." Her heart was dying another death.

"Did I say that?" he thundered.

She hugged her arms to her waist as a defense against his mercurial moods. "Wade," she pleaded with him, "I don't understand you."

He watched her through hooded eyes. "I can relocate my headquarters anywhere I choose, but your parents only have one child. Taking you away from them wouldn't be a good idea."

Heat filled her cheeks. "I'm not nineteen anymore!"

"I've noticed," he murmured as his gaze wandered over her face and body with a raw intensity that left her shaken. "Nevertheless, I wouldn't ask that sacrifice of you."

"But I wouldn't want to deprive you of your family!"

"It's not the same thing," he countered. "With all my business interests in Colorado, we'd see each other on a regular basis. The fact is, I always preferred Salt Lake. The mountains are at your back door. It's smaller, less congested. When I moved here with Dad, I fell in love with the place along with you.''

"You did?" Her voice came out more like a squeak.

"That has never changed."

"But after the way Ty twisted everything—"

"You're asking if I can get past the bad memories enough to live here again?" he broke in, reading her mind.

"Yes."

"That remains to be seen. One thing I do know. I would never show up at that reunion unless you *were* my wife in every sense of the word."

Please, God. Let it happen.

"It—it's not for almost two months," she stammered from excitement she could scarcely suppress. "We could plan a wedding and be married before that date."

His eyes had narrowed on her face. "You must be talking a quiet ceremony at home, then."

"No!" she blurted. "This will be my one and only marriage. I want it at the church, exactly as we planned it before with all our relatives and friends. If we can get the Canyon Inn, then that's where our reception will be."

"Don't weddings on that scale take months to plan?"

"Yes. But since I've had ten years to work out every detail, there's no problem." With that comment, she saw something flicker in the recesses of his eyes. "Nothing has changed but the date, Wade," she rushed to reassure him. "My wedding dress and veil are still hanging in the closet of my bedroom at home. With a few phone calls to your folks and mine, all former plans can be set into motion.

"We'll invite everyone we had on the list except Ty. By the time we go to the reunion, he'll have heard about our nuptials through the fraternity buddies he still pals around with. The news will quash any desire on his part to gloat. He's so mentally disturbed that seeing us married and happy might cause him to reveal what he did. But even if he pretends nothing happened, facing him together will prove cathartic for you and me. We'll be able to get on with our lives and never look back again."

Wade wore a grave expression on his handsome face. "You actually make it sound possible."

"Anything's possible if you want it badly enough," she whispered tearfully.

"Can you put your law practice on hold at a moment's notice like that?"

Was the inquisition never going to stop?

"There are others in the firm who will take over my cases. I want to be there for you every minute, Wade."

"Is that what you really want?"

"How can you even ask me that?" she said in an aching voice. "We've lost ten years. Let's not waste another second of our future together." When he didn't comment, she grew more nervous and said, "Of course, I've just been talking about me. I'm being very selfish. If you would prefer that I continue to work…"

He rubbed his chest unconsciously. "If we were to marry, naturally I would want you to do what makes you happiest."

If…

There was that word again.

Devastated by his guardedness, she asked, "Do you need more time to think about it?"

He eyed her speculatively. "We've been apart ten years. Both of us will have changed a great deal since then."

"I haven't!" she protested. "Not in the ways that count. But apparently you still have reservations." Disheartened, she sensed a remoteness about him.

"Once we're married, there'll be no divorce—no matter what happens."

What could happen? What did he mean?

"You *do* understand what I'm saying."

"Of course," she whispered in fresh anguish because she could find no romance in his soul. In that respect, he *had* changed. Hopefully with marriage and time, she could bring back that joie de vivre she'd thought inherent in his nature. "For better or for worse."

He nodded slowly. "That's right."

As far as she was concerned, they'd already been through the "worse" part. Ten excruciating years of it.

Taking a shallow breath, she said, "Shall we phone our families and tell them the wedding is back on?"

One dark brow dipped lower than the other. "Aren't you afraid a call like that this early in the morning will send your folks into shock?"

Her proud chin lifted. "Not when it's the best news they could ever hear."

He appeared to ponder her comment for a moment, then shrugged his shoulders negligently. "If that's what you want to do."

"It is," she said with marked defiance. "I'd like to talk to your parents, too."

When he didn't respond right away, she cried, "Don't

you? Or is everything moving too fast for you?'' The throb in her voice filled the room.

''If that were the case, I shouldn't have asked you to put this ring on my finger.'' He paused. ''Would that I could reciprocate.'' His brooding expression disturbed her.

''Since I've never been able to wear jewelry, I don't even think about it. You know that. As long as we can live together as man and wife, I'll never ask for anything else again in this life.''

''That's a rather rash statement.'' He sounded amused in a cynical sort of way. ''Which reminds me...before we have to face a barrage of questions from family and friends, we'll have to consider a few practicalities, like where we'll live for the time being.''

It was really going to happen. Her euphoria spilled over into an ecstatic smile.

''That's easy. We can stay right here.''

Before she could blink, he countered with, ''No. That's the one thing we won't do.''

She sucked in her breath, remembering how proud Wade was when it came to taking care of things he considered the man's department.

''Then why don't we leave that decision up to you, and I'll deal with the wedding plans.''

Her suggestion seemed to mollify him. ''Do you own your condo or are you in a lease situation?''

''The latter, but I only have a month to go until it comes up for renewal.''

''That's good.''

"I—I haven't even asked you about your own situation. Is this a bad time to be getting married?"

"I wouldn't care if it was. Bart can handle anything urgent that comes up."

"Is he a good friend?"

Wade nodded. "He and his wife, Linda, are choice people. We've spent a lot of time together. You, particularly, would enjoy her."

"Why is that?"

"She's a former attorney, turned city court judge."

"You're kidding!"

"Getting the three of you together ought to be interesting, to say the least."

"Did you see them socially while you were married to Claire?"

"Yes."

She averted her eyes. This was the hard part...dealing with Wade's past. She would have to learn to cope with the pain if she wanted their marriage to work.

"After we've settled down, we'll have to invite them both to come to Salt Lake for a weekend."

"I'm sure they'd love that."

When nothing else was forthcoming, she moistened her lips. "Wade? How soon do you have to get back to Denver?"

"I should've gone last night with Bart. But obviously something else came up." For a second, his husky voice sounded reminiscent of the old Wade.

"Does that mean you're leaving today?"

"I'm afraid so."

She was frantic. "I wish you didn't have to go. It—it frightens me."

He crossed the expanse separating them and caressed her upper arms through her robe with growing insistence. His thumbs made lazy circles, stirring her senses until she was a trembling mass of feelings.

"Then why don't you come with me? That is, if you can manage to get away."

Her eyelids fluttered closed. "I'll tell Sandy to reschedule my appointments," she said without hesitation.

"In that case, we can tell my family the news together, and you can fly back tomorrow. I'll follow in a few days after I've cleared up some vital business."

"You mean it?"

She was so happy she was afraid this was a dream. To awaken from it would be to die.

His mouth descended swiftly on hers, drawing the very breath from her body. "I'm not particularly fond of a separation from you this soon myself," he muttered against her avid lips. "While I go back to the hotel to pack, why don't you inform your parents of our plans? Ask them if they'll go out to dinner with us next Sunday night."

She could only moan her assent because Wade's mouth was doing the most incredible things to her face and mouth and throat.

"I'll be by for you in two hours," he vowed some time later. She sensed his reluctance to finally put her away from him before he disappeared out the front door of her condo. How he even managed to walk was beyond her comprehension.

The onslaught of his demands had left her shaken and weaving in place. Out of a need for support, she reached for the edge of the nearest end table so she wouldn't collapse in a heap of unassuaged desire only he could satisfy.

While she stood there trying to catch her breath, she heard a sound coming from her guest bedroom. Someone had just sent her a fax. Only a few people had been given her private number. It could be important. Before she phoned her mom and dad, she thought she'd better read it.

Dear J., I have to know. Is the P file permanently open or closed? Whatever the answer, I'm here for you. Love, A.

Janet started to laugh and cry at the same time. *P* stood for *personal*. Whenever she and her best friend had talked about their love life—or the lack of it—they'd always referred to it as the P file.

Before Janet became hysterical with happiness, she faxed Annabelle back.

Dear A. It's permanently open! Wade and I are getting married in a few weeks! You're the first to know. Details to come after I return from Colorado. Tell the big guy I'll love him forever for giving Wade my address.

Love, J.

P.S. I'll love you forever for giving me that pepper spray for Christmas. I accidentally used it on Wade, and one thing led to another. *Capisce*?

Love, J.

P.P.S. It isn't going to be easy. I have to win his trust all over again. It terrifies me.

Love, J.

CHAPTER FIVE

"MAY I help you, sir?"

Wade eyed the hundreds of rings displayed in the glass cases. "I hope so. My fiancée can't tolerate jewelry of any kind if it makes contact with her skin. I'd like to have a pin made for her. One she can wear on her wedding dress. It will have to be a rush order. We're getting married next week."

The older man's eyes lit up. "What an unusual request. Just the kind of challenge that makes me love this business. Do you have anything specific in mind?"

"Only that it be small and exquisite. She's a beautiful, sophisticated woman with impeccable taste. Price is no object."

"Do you have a picture of her?"

His mind conjured up the dozens of photographs and snapshots sitting in the box of memories she'd preserved all these years. *Lord*. Everything about that experience in her condo last week had come close to giving him a heart attack.

"Not with me," he murmured almost as an afterthought.

"Then describe her to me."

That was easy, but when Wade finished listing her physical attributes, he realized you would have to see Janet in person, up close, to fully appreciate the feminine curve of her heart-shaped mouth, the way her eyes

90

blazed with a myriad of tiny blue lights when she grew excited about something.

Her lustrous black hair framed a perfect oval face with features so classic Wade could never take his eyes off them, let alone her long-legged, statuesque figure that had grown more voluptuous with the passage of time.

She'd filled his vision the first time he'd ever seen her in class. Within minutes, she'd taken possession of his heart. There'd been no room for another woman since then.

His guilt over hurting Claire, no matter how unintentional, had dissipated a great deal now that he knew she was happily married to Paul.

Incredibly, Wade could look forward to his own nuptials. In another seven days Janet was going to be his wife. He'd be able to feast his eyes on her for the rest of their lives, knowing he would never tire of the view.

While they'd been making plans for their wedding, the specter of Ty Clark had taken a back seat. In Janet's company, Wade didn't have time to brood about the past. Unfortunately he couldn't prevent certain words and pictures from tormenting his soul whenever they were apart.

Hopefully their marriage would drive out the residue of pain and doubts. More than anything in this world, he wanted to be free to love her as he had once done when he'd been a much younger man. At twenty, he hadn't known what a shadow was. He'd seen no threat to mar their total happiness, not when Janet's love had made him feel immortal.

"I have an idea," the jeweler murmured excitedly, forcing Wade's tortured thoughts back to the business at hand. "Just a moment and let me show you something." He pulled a large picture book out from beneath the counter. It had an old, dull gold cover.

"My grandmother gave me this book upon her return from London years ago after the coronation of King George VI and Queen Elizabeth in 1937. It's the story of the royal family. See these colored pictures of the orb and scepter? Symbols of the church and royal power?"

Wade nodded in fascination at such a wonderful souvenir.

"The first time my eyes beheld all these precious stones, I knew I wanted to be a jeweler when I grew up. See there, above the enormous amethyst of the scepter?" He pointed to what looked like a fleur-de-lis made of diamonds with an emerald-cut emerald in the center.

"How would you like a facsimile made up with an emerald-cut sapphire for its center? The pin would be smaller than a dime, but its brilliance would hold all the fire and catch the eye. It would be one of a kind and fit for a queen, exactly as you have described your beautiful fiancée. She could wear it for any occasion. I would arrange the fastening like a tiepin, easy to attach or remove."

Wade was pleased. In fact, he was more than pleased. Janet wouldn't be expecting anything when it came to the part in the ceremony where he would normally give her a ring. This would be his secret with Pastor Phinney.

"Can you have it ready in six days?"

"I'll give you a phone call in three. You can come and take a look. If you like what you see, then I'll set it for you."

The jeweler's excitement over the project was contagious. Wade left the exclusive Salt Lake store envisioning Janet's reaction with a certain measure of relish. It was only one of several surprises he had in store for her.

Thanks to Cal Rawlins, a friend of Annie's who headed one of the state's largest realty companies, Wade had been able to take possession of a half-finished home being built farther up Emigration Canyon.

The roof had barely been put on the contemporary glass and wood structure erected in a newly opened residential area. It seemed the builder had been forced to abandon the project because of financial difficulties.

When Cal walked Wade through the spacious five-bedroom home and out on the deck, the superb view of the mountains took his breath away. He knew Janet would fall in love with it, too. Her condo at the mouth of the canyon provided mute testimony of her need to be as close to nature as possible.

With all the glass, living in this house would be tantamount to being in the great outdoors year round with all the wonder of Utah's four glorious seasons. Yet they would have their privacy and quick access to the city. The ideal location couldn't have suited their wants and needs better.

Janet had no idea they'd be more or less camping out here after their honeymoon. Together they could finish the house so it became theirs, inside and out.

When the time came, he would have everything he'd put in storage shipped to Salt Lake from Denver. As for her things, a moving van could pack them and bring them up the canyon in one morning. Until their wedding, he would continue to stay at the hotel.

Their exact honeymoon destination he was keeping a

secret. All she knew was that they had to rush their passport applications through, get a few shots and start taking their malaria pills.

The long flight wouldn't be as bad going first class. According to Bart and Linda, what awaited them on the other end would take them out of the world they knew into a fantastic new realm.

That was Wade's goal.

Up until he'd seen Janet again, the world he'd inhabited had, for several reasons, been a hurtful place. He wanted to erase the pain from his memory. Barring that impossibility, he planned to fill their lives with new memories so he wouldn't think.

Thinking had almost destroyed him. If he let his poisonous thoughts persist, they could still destroy him.

"When you walk, the veil floats around you like a white cloud. I've never seen such a heavenly bride. There couldn't be another one as radiant as you, my darling. I'm so thankful Wade came back into your life!"

"Amen, Mom."

Janet smiled in the mirror at her stunning mother, a vision in an off-white, lined silk suit with a treasured strand of pearls, who had just finished arranging the floor-length veil.

Today it was her parents' eyes, not Janet's, that had misted every time they'd looked at her.

At last, this was her wedding day. In a few minutes she was going to be Mrs. Wade Holt. She was too happy, too full of joy, for tears.

The sound of the organ drifted from the nave of the

church to the foyer and into the ante room where she'd been getting ready.

"It's time." Mrs. Larson handed her daughter the spray of white roses and calla lilies with their pale yellow spathes. "Your father's out in the foyer waiting to escort you down the aisle. He's been looking forward to this moment since you first fell in love with Wade."

"I've longed for this day, too." Janet's voice trembled because the waiting was about to come to an end.

"See you in a minute. God bless you, darling." Her mother pressed a kiss to Janet's cheek one more time before leaving the room.

As soon as she found herself alone, she checked to make sure Wade's ring was still fastened to the lace handkerchief she held in her right hand. Satisfied that there was nothing left to do, she took a deep breath and started out the door.

Her tall, distinguished-looking father with wings of gray in his light brown hair beamed when he saw her. She thought he looked splendid in the formal black tux with a white rose pinned to his lapel. Only one man had ever looked better to her.

Just imagining Wade standing in the front of the chapel waiting for her made Janet's heart leap in excitement.

"He's there." Her father read her mind with ease, wanting to reassure her.

Her mouth curved. "I never doubted it. You look wonderful, Dad," she said in a breathless voice.

"Like an overgrown penguin," he quipped. "But this afternoon it doesn't matter because every eye will be on my gorgeous daughter. You know I've always adored you. But have I told you lately how proud I am of you? How much I've admired the way you've handled the good and the bad things life has handed you?''

"*Dad.*" Her father shouldn't have said anything. Now her eyes had started to smart.

"It's true. You've been magnificent through all of it, and today you're being rewarded with your heart's desire. I know it came a little late, but the best things happen to those who have the patience and the fortitude to wait for them. You've been faithful and true. With such a gift, Wade's the luckiest man in the world. All I can say now is, be happy.''

"I am!''

As she leaned forward to hug her father, the organ began playing the processional.

"This is it.'' His light blue eyes twinkled.

She put her arm on top of his and they began the walk she'd waited to take for so many years. The stained-glass windows of the large Presbyterian cathedral filtered the sunlight, bathing the assembled congregation in jewel-like colors.

Though she'd imagined it in her mind many times, she'd never realized what an awesome occasion this would be, nor how meaningful as she passed each pew and saw the faces of everyone she knew smiling back at her with love.

Annie had promised not to cry. But the old saying that promises were made to be broken applied here. Her best friend had been through a lot of pain herself before she and Rand had been reunited.

Her catlike amber eyes seemed to be saying, No more

beach vacations in Florida for us unless it's with our husbands. And then I can guarantee we won't be reading about the latest Washington scandals.

They flashed each other a secret smile before she passed by Cal and a very pregnant Diana Rawlins, who were holding hands. Janet was immediately reminded of Diana's permanent amnesia, a problem that had almost destroyed their marriage. But they'd overcome their difficulties and were happier than ever.

Remembering all these things filled Janet's heart with new hope for her own marriage. As she and her father drew closer to the front of the church, her gaze took in Pastor Phinney wearing his clerical robes, but it quickly fastened on Wade's tall, powerful physique clothed in a formal black dinner suit.

He looked so beautiful in a totally male way that she faltered for a moment. Her father flashed her a knowing grin because he realized she'd just glimpsed the first sight of her husband-to-be.

Those silvery-gray eyes watched her approach from some distance off. The familiar faces of his family and hers became a blur as she looked back at him, wishing she could break tradition and run into his arms.

It seemed to take forever until her father led her to Wade's side and turned away to stand by her mother. One of Wade's married sisters stepped forward to relieve Janet of her flowers. Then she was free to clasp his outstretched hand.

It closed over hers in a possessive grip. When she raised her eyes to his, her body reacted to the blinding intensity of his all-encompassing gaze. Her legs felt as insubstantial as mush.

Wade must have sensed what had happened. As the pastor began the ceremony, he slid his hand beneath her long veil and put a supporting arm around her waist. It was still there when it came time to repeat their vows.

Staring deep into his eyes, she said, "I, Janet Larson, take thee, Wade Holt, to be my lawfully wedded husband. I vow to love thee for better or worse, for richer or poorer, through sickness and health, until death us do part, *and beyond*." She added the last two words in a tremulous voice though they weren't part of the ceremony.

She felt Wade's hand tighten against the curve of her waist before he began in his deep voice, "I, Wade Holt, take thee, Janet Larson, to be my lawfully wedded wife. To have and to hold from this day forward, to love and to cherish. I vow to bestow all my worldly goods on thee, to worship thee with my body, to be thy comfort through sickness and health, for richer or poorer, for better or worse, until death us do part."

"Amen," the pastor said, his eyes smiling kindly at the two of them. "In as much as these two people have sworn their troth, I now pronounce them man and wife, united in the bonds of holy matrimony. What God has bound together, let no man put asunder."

With those last words, the light in Wade's eyes dimmed briefly, causing Janet's heart to plummet. But the moment passed as quickly as it had come.

"Do either of you have tokens you wish to exchange as a symbol of your love?"

"I do," she whispered. Her hands trembled as she pulled the ring from her handkerchief and reached for

Wade's left hand. With a sense of déjà vu, she slid it home.

When she was about to turn back to face the pastor, Wade checked her movement with his hands. Dying of curiosity, she watched him pull something out of his breast pocket.

It was small, bejeweled with what looked like diamonds and a sapphire. They dazzled her eyes, but he moved too quickly for her to see details.

In a gesture she'd never witnessed at anyone's wedding ceremony, he lifted his hands and pinned it to her dress an inch from the neckline above her heart.

"Wade?" she mouthed, inexpressibly thrilled and intrigued by what he'd done.

The tiniest trace of a smile curved one corner of his compelling mouth. A glimpse of the adventurous old Wade broke through. It gave her heart another workout before he gathered her in his strong arms and kissed her mouth with a hunger their guests would notice from the very last pew of the church.

She responded with an eagerness that would make those closest to them blush, but she didn't care. "I love you, my husband," she whispered achingly against his lips, overjoyed that she could finally say those words.

"You're mine now, Janet."

The possessiveness of his tone, threaded with an emotion she couldn't label, caused a voluptuous shiver to course through her body.

"I've always been yours."

She waited for his response, but well-wishers on both sides besieged them, preventing her from hearing what he might have said. The crush of family and friends couldn't be avoided. Everyone wanted to see what he'd pinned on her wedding dress.

No one was more anxious to examine it than she was. When she looked down, she discovered it was a gorgeous fleur-de-lis diamond-and-sapphire pin that she could wear on her clothes instead of sporting a traditional ring. Only Wade would have thought up anything so exquisite and unique.

She couldn't wait to show him in private what his gift meant to her, but right now they had guests to greet. In the excitement, they became separated. She'd just finished hugging Wade's father when she caught sight of someone who hadn't been invited to the wedding.

The shock made her dizzy.

She grabbed on to Wade's mother while she watched Ty leave the rear of the chapel with a group of old fraternity friends. He must have slipped in after the ceremony had started or she would have noticed him during her walk down the aisle with her father.

Dear God. Please don't let Wade have seen him.

But her prayer had come too late.

When she turned around to reach for her new husband, he was staring past her to the rear doors of the chapel where Ty had just passed through.

Those couldn't be Wade's eyes. His irises had darkened until there was no silver left.

Desperate for their wedding day not to be ruined, she threw her arms around his neck. "He's gone, darling," she whispered against his flushed cheek. "Maybe this was the best thing that could have happened. With his own eyes, Ty saw that all his cunning and evil didn't work." Not even seeming to hear her, Wade remained rigidly in place, taut with emotions racking his hard-muscled body. She kissed his ear, biting his lobe gently. "Come on," she urged. "Your father's signaling for us to leave so he can drive us to the reception."

Wade's broad chest rose and fell several times, witness to the terrible struggle he was undergoing to prevent his emotions from erupting in plain view of everyone.

In one last desperate attempt to calm him down, she cupped his face in her hands. After kissing his mouth passionately, she whispered, "He can have no power over us unless we let him." Hopefully any onlookers would think she was telling him sweet nothings.

Another few seconds passed like an eternity before she felt his body relax. His hands began to caress her bare arms below the capped sleeves of her wedding gown, as if he suddenly remembered where he was, who *she* was.

They looked into each other's eyes. For the time being, the savage glaze had abated. In its place she saw that fragile look of vulnerability once more.

Damn you, Ty, for bringing it back today of all days.

But Janet wasn't about to let him inflict any more damage if she could help it.

"I don't know about *you*, Mr. Holt, but your new wife can't hold out much longer for her wedding night." She ran her hands up his shirt-covered chest inside his suit jacket. "If we're going to have one before this day is over, then we have to follow through with the reception first. What do you say we get this show on the road as quickly as possible?"

Her words, her touch—maybe a combination of both—ignited something inside Wade. She heard his breath catch before he lowered his mouth to hers one more time.

"I'm ready, Mrs. Holt."

The ardor of his kiss convinced her he was equally impatient to get her alone. Thankful he'd pulled out of the worst of the black rage that had swept over him, she put her arm through his and let him guide them toward the church exit.

Half their friends still lingered to take pictures of the bridal couple as they emerged from the cathedral and headed to the car parked in front where Wade's father was waiting.

Once they were ensconced in the back seat of his dad's Audi—a difficult feat with all her wedding finery—she put her hand behind Wade's neck and kissed him again. "This pin is the most incredible piece of jewelry I've ever seen in my life. Where did you find it? I adore it!"

His eyes had softened to a somber gray color. "I had it specially made for you." With a little coaxing, he proceeded to tell her the history behind it.

"I'm going to find a way to wear it every day of my life."

A chuckle came out of Wade. After what had just happened inside the church, she didn't think that was possible.

"Why do you laugh?"

"I'm afraid you're going to have problems, my love. We're married now. As your husband, I plan to keep you in a state of undress more often than not."

"Wade—"

"Don't tell me you're shocked."

"No." She buried her face in his neck. "I'm afraid you're going to be the one who's shocked to find out your new bride is anything but shy. I've spent too many years imagining what it would be like to belong to you. In case you didn't realize that, I'm warning you now."

This time, he laughed out loud. It was a heavenly sound. The unpleasantness hadn't marred the day after all.

"Most men have a fantasy, but only rarely, if ever, does it become attainable." He kissed her around the mouth, teasing, provoking her until she moaned in frustration. "It seems the gods decided they've punished me long enough and deigned to grant me the wish of my heart."

In the next breath, his mouth covered hers. She was lost.... Not until Wade's father let them know they'd arrived at the Canyon Inn did she become cognizant of her surroundings.

Sounds of the rushing mountain stream greeted her ears. The air was cooler. "I can't believe we're here already." She tried to smooth her hair into some semblance of order, but it was a lost cause. "Everyone's going to know what we've been doing," she moaned in panic.

While his attractive father smiled, Wade's shoulders shook with silent laughter.

"This isn't funny, darling! Mom has my purse with her. We can't start pictures until I've freshened up in the rest room. My veil has slipped. Hide me," she begged as he helped her from the car and rushed her through the side entrance where there weren't many people.

Twenty minutes later, she'd put herself back together, the photographer had finished taking pictures for their wedding album and they were ready to greet their guests.

Janet didn't believe Ty had the temerity to show up at their reception uninvited, but she remained on tenterhooks for the next two hours all the same. Though they never mentioned his name, she knew Wade had been keeping a watchful eye for any sign of him, as well.

When it was time to cut the cake, she was relieved beyond belief that he hadn't made an appearance. Feeling more relaxed, she thoroughly enjoyed feeding Wade his piece of cake. She loved watching him under every circumstance. Her heart lodged in her throat when she realized that as his wife she now had the right to continue watching him, loving him, for the rest of her life.

Wade flashed her an enigmatic glance, then cut the next piece. But instead of putting the whole thing in her mouth as she'd anticipated, he ate it himself. A roar of laughter broke out among their guests.

"I'd rather kiss you than feed you, Mrs. Holt." His comment brought a deep blush to her neck and face before he drew her into his arms and proceeded to do just that until she was breathless.

In the background, she heard men's voices break into song. Some of the alums from the fraternity had formed a semicircle to serenade them.

"Did you plan this?" Wade muttered against her ear.

"No," she whispered back in alarm. "I promise you this is something they decided to do themselves. But I'm not surprised. You were always well liked by everyone." *Despite anything Ty told you otherwise.*

After three songs, Lex and Art, two of Wade's former roommates at the fraternity house, approached. She felt him stiffen.

"Congratulations, you two," Lex said heartily. "When I heard you had broken up years ago, I couldn't believe it. Whatever happened, it's great to see you back together again where you obviously belong. Are you going to be living in Denver?"

"No. Salt Lake," Wade said without embellishment.

"That's terrific. Then let's get together one of these days soon. I'm in the phone book."

"So am I," Art piped up. "We play handball after work a couple of times a month. You've got to come and show us how it's done. Let's face it. You always were better than everybody else."

"I'll call you."

Wade's aloof demeanor wounded her. By the tone of his voice, Janet could tell he thought the other men had condescended to make small talk because it was expected of them.

"If you don't, we'll phone *you*," Lex vowed. "But we'll give you a little time with Miss America here first. Everyone knows what a damn lucky man you are," he said within hearing distance before he winked at Janet and patted Wade on the shoulder.

Wade's expression remained inscrutable as he watched them melt into the crowd.

Janet had felt their sincerity. Surely Wade had, too! "Darling—"

"Are you ready to go?" The question cloaked a demand. She thought she understood. Too many painful memories of the past were choking him. If Ty hadn't shown up at the wedding, Wade might not have been upset.

"I'm ready now," she whispered, falling in with his wishes.

She tossed her bouquet and they said their goodbyes. Wade clasped her hand and they made their getaway. But the unnatural quiet coming from his side of the rental car on the drive down the canyon was so different from the way he'd acted on the way up that she couldn't relate to the stranger behind the wheel.

He pulled the car around the back of her parents' home. "Is there anything else you need to do besides change clothes?" The quiet question came after he'd helped her out of the car.

"No. You took care of my bags earlier."

Wade stood there with his legs slightly apart, his hands in his pockets. "Do you need help with your dress?"

Her eyes closed tightly. He was still in too much pain to shake it off. "No."

"Then do you mind if I wait out here for you? I want to make a last minute call about our flight on my cell phone."

"Of course I don't mind. I'll be right back."

As she turned to leave, he caught her in his arms. "Janet… Forgive me" came his tortured plea before he kissed her long and hard on the mouth.

His torment, combined with his passion, revealed the extent of his vulnerability and made her love him that much more. With obvious reluctance, he finally released her.

"I'll hurry," she promised as she dashed inside the

house and raced upstairs to her old room. It didn't take long to remove her wedding paraphernalia. The sooner they got on their honeymoon, the sooner they would make new memories and leave Ty in the dust where he belonged.

She dressed in a new white, two-piece cotton suit, determined to show Wade her understanding, not her tears.

Seeing his old fraternity brothers again must have been like walking barefoot on hot coals. Every comment could be misconstrued if you'd lost trust and were looking for innuendo....

She removed the precious diamond-and-sapphire pin from her wedding dress and attached it securely to the lapel of her suit. After slipping on her sandals, she reached for her purse, then ran downstairs and out the back door, determined to comfort her beloved husband no matter how long it took.

CHAPTER SIX

ANOTHER animal's death cry filled the predawn air, bringing Wade awake.

After two weeks on safari in Kenya, he was more fascinated than ever by every sight and sound coming from the bush that surrounded their tent, if you could call it that. It had every amenity: modern bathroom with hot and cold running water, dark antique furniture, a comfortable double bed with a canopy of mosquito netting.

In a move as automatic as breathing, he reached for his wife who slept quietly beside him. When he gathered her to his body so her back rested against his chest and her long, smooth legs tangled with his hair-roughened limbs, she made a small sound of contentment but slept on.

This was their last night in Africa. They'd made love for most of it, their needs primitive and insatiable. At some point, they'd fallen asleep, exhausted. But now he was awake again, wanting a repeat performance.

Wade had known he'd married a passionate woman, but he never dreamed she would be the kind of exciting, unselfish lover who went on giving and giving until she made him feel immortal.

He buried his face in her glorious black hair. The glossy strands spread the scent of peaches all over him and the pillows. For the rest of their lives he would always associate this particular fragrance with their honeymoon.

Until now, every second, every minute had been idyllic. He'd managed to shove all black thoughts to a corner of his mind and concentrate fully on his beautiful, breathtaking wife. Here in the bush there'd been no shadows to mar their bliss. Their joy in each other knew no limits.

But tomorrow they had to go home.

He stared into the darkness, dreading the prospect because Janet was opposed to a confrontation with Ty, and Wade knew there was going to be one.

She wanted the ugliness of the past to go away like a bad dream. On their drive to the airport the night of the wedding, she'd begged him to forget the past. "Ty can't hurt us anymore. We're married now. That's all that matters, darling."

But it wasn't all that mattered.

Wade couldn't let it go if he'd wanted to. Lex's comments at the reception had only fanned the scorching flames of doubt that threatened to destroy the new foundation of love Wade had started building with her.

Out of deference for his wife's feelings, he'd been putting off the inevitable. But now that they were married, he refused to wait any longer.

"Darling?"

"You're awake?" he whispered huskily.

In a lightning move, she turned over so that she lay in his arms facing him. "Something's wrong. I could feel you start to breathe hard. I thought maybe you were having a bad dream."

They'd gotten so close they were keyed into each other's deepest thoughts and feelings.

He caressed her face with his lips, lingering much longer at her mouth. "To be honest, I can't fathom leaving Kenya."

"Neither can I!" she cried, returning kiss for kiss. "We've been transported to such a different and beautiful world I can't believe it's still part of our planet. Promise me we can come back again in a few months! We've only seen such a little bit of the country so far. It's more than fabulous. In fact, it's impossible to describe."

"Now you know how I feel about being your husband. What you do to me is impossible to describe." He rolled on top of her. "Love me, Janet," he said, his voice shaking. He began kissing her with refined savagery. "I need you now more than I ever have in my life."

"You *are* my life," she declared tremulously. Wrapping her arms around his neck, she implored, "Give me a baby."

A groan of ecstasy escaped his throat as he set about to grant his wife her wish. An hour later, when they had both been temporarily sated, she'd fallen asleep in his arms once more.

He nibbled on her shoulder, hoping he'd made her pregnant here in the bush. Because of her mother's history, Janet worried about her own ability to conceive.

If ever a woman was ready to become a mother, it was she.

Yesterday they'd flown to the Masai-Mara. There on the patio of the main lodge overlooking the river, they'd been served eggs Benedict while they'd watched four noisy hippos lounging on the banks. Their rotund size and eerie laughter were a constant source of amazement.

Janet couldn't take enough pictures of the huge baby hippo who lay by his mother, too fat to crawl on her. It was quite a different scene from the pride of lions they'd passed late that afternoon in their open-roofed, four-wheel-drive vehicle.

In the tall grass of the Serengeti, the roly-poly cubs pummeled their mother and rolled around playfully with her. Their activity delighted Janet. She begged the guide to let them stay parked longer in order to record every sound and movement.

Everywhere they went, she wanted to linger around the mothers with their young. Two days ago, they'd come across some adult female giraffes feeding from the tops of the prickly pear trees while their babies pressed close to them and ate from the branches lower down.

When Wade looked over at his wife, tears were streaming from her deep blue eyes. "Isn't that the most beautiful, amazing sight you ever saw?"

He agreed the animal life was spectacular. But there could be no more breathtaking view than the one before him. Her face was bathed in the rays of a setting sun just before the orange ball disappeared behind Mt. Kenya.

It wasn't just her outward beauty, those black-fringed eyes and long, flowing hair, or even the delicate arch of perfectly shaped brows and lips. His brilliant wife was beautiful inside, always kind and genteel, yet unafraid to show a child's delight in everything she saw.

What a damn lucky man you are.

Wade knew how lucky he was and didn't need any reminders. Especially not from Lex, who believed Ty had gotten there first with Janet and couldn't resist baiting him.

It had been next to impossible to stand there with his bride while the guys serenaded them and pretend he didn't know what was going on in all their minds.

The speed with which Wade had dropped out of the fraternity and left the campus would only have added credence to Ty's lies. Coupled with what Janet had told him about Ty's constant attention to her after Wade had left Salt Lake, the whole affair must have been the fraternity's most talked-about scandal.

Janet had overridden Wade's desire not to invite any of them to the wedding. She insisted on including them because she wanted to show him she had nothing to hide. Against his better judgment, he'd finally caved in. But he knew the only reason they'd decided to sing was to satisfy their inherent curiosity.

It surprised Wade that Ty hadn't crashed the reception after showing up persona non grata at the wedding. This time, no amount of pleading on Janet's part would change Wade's mind about going after him once they'd returned to Salt Lake.

He had a plan. First, however, he needed some advice from Rand. Normally he would have asked Annie, but she was too closely aligned to Janet. Wade didn't want to put Annie in the position of having to keep secrets from her best friend.

"Wade?" Janet sat up in the bed and cupped his face

with her hands. He could feel her anxiety. "There's something bothering you. I have to know what it is."

"Very simply, I don't want to go home." That, at least, wasn't a lie. He reached for her hands and kissed the palms.

"Neither do I. I've been so happy here, I never want it to end."

"It's not over yet!" Gathering his wife in his arms, he headed for the shower. "We're not due to take the plane back to Nairobi for another hour. I want to concentrate on you until the very last second. I swear I'll never be able to get enough of you."

"Obviously your honeymoon was everything you dreamed it would be. Why not come in the dining room, darling? Dozens of wedding presents arrived while you were away. I've put them on the table." Janet's mother slipped her arm through her daughter's as they walked through the house together.

Before the wedding, she and Wade had already opened dozens of gifts. Now there was a new pile.

"I think I'll load up my car and we'll open them together tonight."

With her mother's help, they made short work of it.

"Where is Wade?" she asked after Janet had gotten back in her car.

"As soon as we reached the house, he phoned Bart and they've been going strong ever since. I thought this would be the best time to visit you."

"I'm so thrilled you came. I've missed you." She leaned inside and gave her daughter another hug. "I'm just sorry your father wasn't here. If you and Wade can arrange it, come for dinner tomorrow night.''

"We'd love to! You won't believe the videos we took. Oh, Mom I'm so happy, I'm frightened.''

Her mother frowned. "Frightened?''

"Yes. Wade was like a different person in Kenya. But now that we're back, I'm afraid he's brooding over what Ty did to us. I had hoped we could put all that behind us, but Ty's unexpected appearance at the wedding upset him horribly. I just couldn't bear it if there was any trouble now.''

Her mother eyed her with concern. "Your father and I were shocked about that, too. Remember that Wade's pride was hurt along with his broken heart. Sometimes men have a little harder time getting over things. They brood, as you say, while women tend to talk and talk about it until they work it out of their systems.''

Janet clutched the steering wheel tightly. "Wade is a master at keeping his demons to himself.''

"Your father was a lot like that when we were first married. It took a long time to mellow him to the point that he would talk things out with me.''

Janet eyed her mother shrewdly. "So what you're saying is, there's hope.''

"Of course there is.'' She kissed her cheek. "You've just come back from a dream honeymoon. Now the real work begins.''

"Wade's my major priority from now on. Did I tell you that I'm taking time away from the office for an indefinite period?''

"Yes. I think it's a wonderful idea. With a beautiful

new house to finish decorating and a yard to put in, I'd say you have more than enough on your plate."

Janet stared at her mother. "I'm not as young as I used to be. I want a baby right away."

"I want that for you, too, darling."

"Thank you, Mom. I love you."

"I love you, too. Give Wade a welcome-home hug for me."

"I will."

"See you tomorrow night?"

"Yes."

She backed out of the driveway, waving once more to her mother before she drove off. While she traveled along the freeway, she mulled over her mother's admission about her father's inability to open up when they'd first gotten married.

Janet couldn't remember a time when her parents didn't talk everything over, even into the long hours of the night. Obviously her father had changed a great deal since being a newlywed.

The knowledge made Janet more determined than ever that one day she and Wade were going to have the same kind of marriage as her parents. With enough love and encouragement, she would get Wade to talk about his thoughts and feelings.

Right now, he had a pattern of making love to her when he wanted the discussion closed. Not that she was complaining. His lovemaking was a miracle she could never get enough of. But there were times when she knew that despite their physical closeness, his dark thoughts persisted in haunting him long after he'd believed she'd gone to sleep. If she had anything to say about it, one day soon that was going to change.

Before starting up the canyon, she glanced at her watch. It was close to dinnertime. Wade would be starving and their kitchen wasn't in order yet. She decided to pick up Chinese at a local restaurant and surprise him.

But in the end she was the one surprised and disappointed when she reached the fantastic home Wade had bought for them only to discover his new Saab was missing.

He'd left a message on the utility island in the middle of their kitchen. "My love—I needed to run a few errands. Should be home by seven at the latest. I'll bring dinner with me."

She crushed the note in her hand, wondering what errands were so important they couldn't wait until she'd returned so they could do them together.

Stop it, Janet. Wade had lived ten years without her. Just because they were married didn't give her the right to smother him.

Angry over her own battle with paranoia, she tossed the note in the box they were using as a waste bin. Day after tomorrow, the movers would come with her things. On Wednesday of next week, a moving van would arrive with Wade's belongings. Once everything had been delivered, they would mix it all together and see what else was needed to turn this house into *their* home.

Secretly she couldn't wait to find out what kind of taste he had in furnishings while he'd lived at his condo in Denver. When they were nineteen, she thought she knew everything about him. But he was a thirty-year-old man now. There were many things still to be discovered. She felt breathless just anticipating life with him over the next fifty years. Or sixty if they were really lucky.

Delirious with happiness because she was finally his wife, she put the food in the fridge, then hurried through to the laundry room to start a wash. With all the clothes she and Wade had worn on safari, it would take the whole evening to get it done.

A half hour later in their bedroom, she was startled when she felt a pair of masculine hands make wayward movements over her hips. "Well, well—" his lips found her tender neck "—who's this gorgeous body folding all my clothes into neat little piles?"

She whirled around in his arms. Smiling up into his handsome face, she said, "I'm the new woman of the house. Whatever you want—anything you want—I'm here to provide. All day long. All night long."

When he wanted her, his silvery eyes smoldered with desire. Right now, they looked like they could start a bonfire. "You mean if I asked you to stop what you're doing and lie down on the bed with me this instant, you would do it?"

"I was afraid you would never ask." Without giving him warning, she fell backward on the bed and pulled him on top of her. "You did say this instant."

He broke into deep laughter before rolling them around on their new king-size bed. The clothes flew everywhere.

"I'm afraid your neat little piles are no more," he whispered against her lips before devouring her inch by inch. The volatile chemistry between them took over.

Much later, Wade put on a pair of cutoffs and threw

her his robe. Together they headed for the kitchen to eat dinner. He'd brought Chinese, as well. They chuckled before she mixed both meals together and served them on the deck where they'd put some lounging chairs.

It was one of those balmy June nights when you could hear the crickets and smell honeysuckle in the air. She took a deep breath. "Hmm. Summer in Salt Lake."

"There's nothing like it. Not even in the Masai-Mara."

She swallowed the rest of her egg roll. "Wade..." she began tremulously. "Thank you for our honey-moon."

"You already have. A hundred times at least."

"I—I know. But it was perfect."

"I agree. That's because you were there."

"I love you so much it hurts."

"Tell me about it."

"Sometimes I think this is still a dream and I'm going to wake up. I couldn't handle it if I lost you now."

"I'm not going anywhere."

"It was just a figure of speech, darling. You *know* what I meant."

"I do," he answered sincerely.

"Mom and Dad have invited us for dinner tomorrow night. Is that all right with you?"

"I'm looking forward to it."

"They can't wait to see our videos. Neither can I."

Desire lit his eyes. "Maybe we shouldn't watch them yet. I'm already halfway determined to take us back to Kenya on the next plane."

"No one ever had a honeymoon like ours," she said, her voice quivering before she got to her feet and took their paper plates in the house. Wade followed with their empty soda cans.

"I see more presents have arrived."

"Yes. Shall we open them now?"

He flashed her a wicked smile. "Maybe a couple. I had planned on an early night with you."

"In that case, I'll only pick one."

Her glance darted to the various packages. The majority of them looked like the china they'd registered at various stores. One smaller square box looked interesting. She reached for it.

Once she'd opened the carton, she felt around in the pellets for the paper-wrapped object. After unraveling it, she discovered a white ceramic seagull. She flicked Wade a puzzled gaze.

His lips twitched. "Just what we always wanted."

That small trace of a smile made her heart rate quicken. "Maybe it's from someone in the state government. The seagull is our state bird after all."

"Isn't there a card?"

"I'm looking for it." She dipped her hand inside once more and caught the edge of the envelope with her fingernails. "It has your name on it."

"I don't know anyone in the government," he quipped. "You open it for me."

"Men," she teased. In a second, she'd slit it open. There was no name, only a short note.

"May this bird find a place among your treasured objects to constantly remind you of your pure white bride."

When the message sank in, sickness welled in her throat. Praying for strength, she said, "This is just a note from the store saying that they couldn't find the note and would research it.''

There was no way to escape Wade's piercing gaze. ''You're lying.''

''Why would I do that?''

''Your face has turned ashen.''

''I—I think the Chinese food has made me sick.''

She flew from the kitchen to the bathroom adjoining their bedroom. To her horror, there was no lock on the door.

Her hands shook as she tore the paper into several pieces and threw them in the toilet. But just as she was about to flush it, a bronzed hand reached out to prevent her. As he was so much stronger than she was, there was no contest.

In the next instance, he'd fished the pieces from the water. She followed him into the bedroom where he sank onto the bed and started piecing the scraps together.

When he raised his head, she had trouble recognizing her husband. His face had become an expressionless mask.

He levered himself from the bed. ''Why couldn't you have shown this to me?''

She swallowed hard. ''Because I knew it would upset you, and we've barely come back from a heavenly honeymoon.''

''I don't think that's the real reason.''

''What other one could there be?''

He sucked in his breath. ''Fear.''

''You're right. I'm always afraid of your reaction when it comes to the past.''

"You mean when it comes to Ty. Why don't you just say his name?"

"Because I abhor what he did to us. What he's still doing," she said through gritted teeth. "Obviously our not inviting him to the wedding fueled his anger. In retaliation, he sent that bird as a sick joke. Wouldn't he enjoy it if he could see us right now, practically at each other's throat?"

His eyes had gone bleak once more. "You ran away from me."

"I told you why. Do you think my conscience got the best of me, is that it?"

The silence lengthened. He moved to the bathroom to wash his hands.

"I asked you a question, Wade. I'd like an answer. Do you still believe I slept with him?"

Slowly he began drying his hands with one of the towels. The deathly quiet was murdering her soul.

Wade stood there clutching the towel in his hands. Since their marriage, she'd returned every cruel salvo he'd fired at her with a demonstration of unqualified love. Never by word or deed had she given him reason to be jealous. Not ten years ago. Not now.

No one in this world could have a more loving, caring spouse than he did. If someone came to him this minute and asked him what more she could do to prove herself, he would have to answer, "Nothing." She was perfect.

In the end, it always came down to Ty's word against hers.

By their fruits ye shall know them.

She'd never presented anything but good fruit.

Ty had never presented anything but bad.

He groaned as another more damning indictment against him tortured his conscience.

All this time, all these years, he'd been fixated on his own pain. Never once had he really thought about Janet's. Those five weeks of phone calls from her after he'd gone back to Denver hadn't been able to penetrate his wounded psyche. He'd been impervious to her agony.

His mother, the one other person in his life he'd been unable to forgive, had been forced to stand by helplessly while her son deliberately sabotaged any effort Janet made to meet and talk about their broken engagement.

At the zenith of his pain, he'd actually taken delight in hearing her great heaving sobs over the telephone. The more she begged and pleaded, the more pleasure he took in repudiating her.

But somehow those sobs had made their way past his defenses. Ten years later they were reverberating in his soul with a great howling cry that wrenched his gut.

There was no way around the fact that her suffering had been exquisite. The box of memories had proved that beyond any doubt.

Everything she'd ever done had been out of love for him. No matter how abominably he treated her, she returned it with a greater measure of love. She never reviled him, never played the payback game. It wasn't in her nature.

As awful as he'd been to her the night he'd waited by the entrance to her condo, she'd been so worried about injuring his eyes that she'd taken no thought for herself.

Her one and only desire had been to nurse him, take care of him.

He blinked back the tears.

How long do you intend to inflict punishment on her?

After all these years, Wade finally knew the answer to that question. Unequivocally. Ty Clark was the liar, not Janet.

"No, darling. I don't believe a word he said. But certain fears die hard." His dark head reared back. "Did I ever tell you about my mother's affair?"

When the words registered, the staggering revelation presented Janet with a whole new set of circumstances she would never have imagined.

"It took my being married the first time to understand why my dad suspected something was wrong in their marriage. When you live with someone day and night, you notice all the little things, a change in mood or demeanor.

"Dad could tell Mom wasn't as responsive, so he asked her if she'd been with another man. She said no. She swore she'd been a faithful wife."

Janet's eyes closed in pain.

"Two jobs later, plus a drinking binge that put him in the hospital, she could see the damage her lies had caused. In a moment of truth, she finally admitted there'd been this doctor. But it had only lasted a couple of weeks because she realized she was still in love with Dad and didn't want a separation."

"Oh, Wade..."

"Dad lost it. He was gone for a couple of months. When he came back, he said he wanted a divorce. All my mother did was cry."

And you cried, my darling.

"She begged him not to leave her, but he filed anyway. Mom pleaded with me to make him see reason. Of course, I couldn't do anything. He was too far gone. You'll never know how helpless I felt watching my parents' marriage fall apart. If you could have heard Dad…

"'The thing about it is this, son. I could handle the fact that your mother had been with another man. Lord knows I had been with two other women I thought I was in love with before I married her. But being married is different.

"'I'm not saying her affair didn't hurt like hell or that it wouldn't always hurt somewhere in my heart. But I figured I could live with it because I loved her too much to lose her.

"'The thing that made it so hard was the lying. Through that period, life was a living hell. The old expression, "The truth shall make you free", wasn't coined without a reason.'

"That's when Dad told me he was moving to Salt Lake, to try to build another life. The tension was so bad around the house it sounded like a good idea to me. I decided to go with him."

Janet stood there shaking her head. "Wade…why didn't you tell me about this after we started dating?"

His jaw hardened. "I couldn't. I was too angry and felt betrayed by my mom. I could understand why Dad was in agony. From that point on it was a love-hate relationship with her.

"During the period Dad and I lived together, he had time to do a lot of thinking. So did Mom. She begged for a reconciliation. One day a year later, just before college started, he sat me down.

"'Son,' he said, 'it's taken me a long time to come around, but your mom did break down and tell the truth. So I've decided to go back to her. We're going to have to work harder than ever at our marriage to make it good, but this time we'll have honesty going for us. That's what will make all the difference.'"

"I remember how shocked I was, Janet. I tried to put myself in my father's place. If it had been my wife, and she'd finally told me the truth, I asked myself if it would have been any easier to hear the words. If she did say them, would I have been able to forgive her and stay in the marriage like my father?

"The more I thought about it, the more I realized I wasn't anything like Dad. I knew myself too well. If I were married, and my wife ever admitted she'd been unfaithful and had lied to me about it, I would have left her in a heartbeat and never looked back."

"Darling—"

"As you can imagine, I didn't have much hope for my parents, but I supported anything they tried to do. I know my sisters were ecstatic. By that time, I was planning to marry you. Naturally it distanced me from their problems, which they eventually solved."

She stared at him through the tears. "Now that you've told me all this, I understand completely why you refused to talk to me!" she cried out. "If I had known this from the beginning, I would have realized what was happening and I would have flown to Denver anyway." She buried her face in her hands. "Why did Ty have to come into our lives?"

"I've asked myself that question more times than you have. But the answer is always the same. Because he was there first."

"But he never had anything to do with my life!" she insisted. "Wade... I went on a couple of dates with him. That's all! Everybody dated everybody. It didn't mean anything. I had no special feelings for him. You know I didn't. You were in class with us. I was so crazy about you it's a miracle I didn't fail debate."

"What about when you were younger?"

"That would make us children. We did have the same piano teacher for a few years and we were on the same swim team during the summers."

He eyed her intently from beneath furrowed brows. "Did you ever give him any reason to think the two of you might end up together one day?"

She started to say no, then thought of something.

"What?" Wade had an uncanny ability to read her mind.

"During our junior year of high school, I was voted in as queen for the Christmas dance. Ty was voted in as king. It's tradition that the king and queen and their attendants also voted in have to go to the dance together. A lot of comments were made that night about our being the perfect couple. It was ridiculous, and I paid absolutely no attention to it. But—"

"But that might have been when his obsession with you started," he stated the obvious.

"Maybe..." her voice trailed off. "D-do you think his feelings for me border on obsession?"

"I don't know. I'm not a psychiatrist. The fact that Ty finally gave up on you and married another girl sounds like he got over you. But coming to our wedding uninvited makes me wonder if those feelings were always there, simmering beneath the surface. As long as you weren't married to anyone else, he could handle it. But when he found out about you and me, he became actively disturbed again. Rand thinks it's a possibility.''

''Rand?''

''I met him for lunch today.''

That was his errand? She blinked. ''Was Annie with you?''

''No. I asked him to come alone and not tell her.''

''I see.''

''No, you don't. You and Annie are too close. She loves you too much. I needed the opinion of someone who's able to be a little bit more objective.''

''Do you think he's been stalking me all these years?'' The mere idea sent a shudder through her body.

''I doubt it,'' Wade mused aloud. ''He wouldn't have to resort to that. Not when you have mutual friends. But this bird…'' He eyed it as if it were something evil. ''It's something else again. I want Rand to see the note.''

''If this is a stalking case, he'll take it to their boss, Roman.''

''I remember you telling me about him. Isn't he the P.I. who caught the man stalking his wife?''

Janet nodded. ''It was awful. Lindsay hired Roman to protect her. They fell in love while he worked under cover as her pretend husband. After that maniac was arrested, she and Roman got married.''

Wade pursed his lips. ''I don't know if Ty could be classified as a maniac. On the surface, he looks like the kind of clean-cut, preppy guy every mother would love to claim for her son. But he must be devoid of a conscience and doesn't function along normal lines."

"It's so sad," she murmured. "His father is revered and has always been in politics. Recently he was elected to the Utah House of Representatives. The Clarks are very social people. Ty has an older brother who got married a long time ago. It makes you wonder if he's been neglected emotionally."

Just then their phone rang.

"Rand was going to do a little background check on him to find out. Maybe he's calling back right now with some information." Wade reached for the receiver and said hello.

Janet moved closer.

"Annie!...It's good to hear your voice, too.... No, you're not bothering us. You could never do that. As a matter of fact, we just started opening wedding presents. My other half is right here dying to talk to you. I'll put her on."

"Don't go anywhere," she whispered anxiously as he handed her the receiver. "I won't stay on long."

"I'm just going to lock up." He pressed a swift kiss to her lips before leaving the room.

CHAPTER SEVEN

As soon as Janet took the phone from him, Wade gathered the pieces of paper from off the bed and headed for the kitchen. When he found the box, he put the seagull back in it along with the ripped-up note.

What he'd really like to do was ram the damn bird down Ty's throat. Barring that, he would put everything in the Dunbartons' capable hands and let them come up with a plan to expose Ty.

Because it was Annie, Wade figured his wife would be on the phone for a while. Now would probably be a good time to move the paint cans from the garage into the downstairs family room so it would be ready for the painters tomorrow. The upstairs walls had been painted and the woodwork finished the way he and Janet had planned, but the lower level of the house still wasn't done.

Full of too much excess energy, Wade arranged everything for the workmen, then made a tour of the entire house, checking windows and doors to be sure all was secure before going to bed.

Was it only three nights ago he didn't have a care in the world while he made sweet, languorous love to his adorable wife deep in the heart of Africa? Could there be a sweeter, more responsive or spontaneous woman anywhere?

After shutting the sliding glass door to the deck and

locking it, Wade stood in the dark, scoring his hair with his hands. From the beginning, Janet had maintained her innocence, but he hadn't been truly convinced until their honeymoon.

What bothered him was that he had needed any proof. In that regard, he had hurt Janet deeply. She was still hurting, otherwise he wouldn't be able to hear her sobs coming from the bedroom.

The sound wrenched his gut. There'd been too much pain. Wade needed to turn things around starting tonight.

Silently Wade moved through the bedroom to the bathroom and showered. A few minutes later, he joined his wife in bed, desperate to quiet her tears and prove to her that old wounds could heal, that they could have a beautiful life together from here on out.

The second she felt him crawl under the covers, she turned toward him. He reached for her eagerly and pulled her firmly against his body. Letting out a heavy sigh, he said, "If you were to talk to my mother, she would tell you I always did react first and repent later."

He kissed her shoulder. "It's one of my worst faults, which are too many to list tonight. But I'm going to make you one promise. I'll never run away from a problem facing us again. Never," he whispered against her hot cheek. "I swear it."

"I won't, either," she declared. "Darling... I told Annie what you talked to Rand about today. She thinks we have everything figured out wrong."

Wade played with a tendril of silky hair that swirled on her neck. "That sounds like our Annie. The most independent thinker I ever met."

"That's why Roman Lufka hired her to work for his

agency. A genius with added feminine intuition. She's been doing her own research on the side and believes Ty has a psychotic hatred of you that started the first day you came to debate class."

Wade's hand spanned her neck and throat. "I remember that day as if it were yesterday. Ty looked at me after the debate coach made our team assignments. If his eyes had been lethal weapons, I'd be dead by now." He felt her shiver as if it had originated from his own body.

"The first football game Annie and I attended to watch you play, she found out from one of the team members that the head coach let you start at your position instead of Ty. Apparently you did so much better in practice than he did that Ty was benched most of the season. It's no wonder you ended up all-state linebacker for our high school's region. You lied to Annie and me when you said you would probably have to sit out most of the year because you'd come late to Salt Lake!"

Unable to resist, Wade kissed her well-shaped nose. "I didn't know you found out that stuff about me."

"I wanted to know everything about you," she said in a trembling voice. "Luckily I had Annie to do all my dirty work. She was a natural sleuth. I should have known that one day she would end up as a P.I."

Delighted by his wife's unexpected confession, he moved his leg over hers, drawing her more firmly against him. "What else don't I know that you're going to tell me?" he whispered against her temple where he could feel a pulse throbbing madly. He heard her expel a sigh.

"Annie looked up some information and found out that Ty's brother was an all-state football player when he was in high school."

"I had no idea how much was riding on Ty's desire to play the position."

"There's more," she said. "Do you remember Ty telling everyone that he'd passed up a couple of scholarships for schools back east in order to attend the University of Utah on scholarship?"

"I guess I do. But you were the focal point of my existence. Everything else was just so much background."

"Well, Annie went to work in her inimitable way. For one thing, she discovered that you got a 33 on your SAT scores. Ty only had a 21. She also learned that he wasn't accepted at any schools back east, let alone given scholarships. He applied to the University of Utah and was accepted, but not on scholarship. Maybe you didn't know this, but his dad, the former governor, was a top honors graduate of Princeton University."

"So Annie has deduced that he's been in competition all his life."

"Yes. She thinks that because he knew me first and had dated me, he felt a certain sense of ownership."

"Until I came along and took you away from him."

"Something like that. Little by little, he focused all his frustration and jealousy on you because you represented everything he wasn't."

Wade buried his face in her hair. "If her theory is true, then it would have been hard to follow the progress of our relationship."

"Exactly. Annie believes the night we announced our engagement at the winter fest formal dance, it was the turning point and he went over the edge. It was right after that when you flew to Denver to talk to your parents. He saw an opportunity to strike out at supposed injustices to him and took it without regard for the consequences."

"Annie could be right on all counts."

"I told her about the note he sent with the seagull. That alarmed her. She has a warning for you."

"What's that?" he murmured, making inroads to her lips.

"You're not to go anywhere near Ty, not until she's talked everything over with Rand and Roman. They'll get back to us."

"She thinks he's dangerous?"

"Yes. So do I. Promise me you won't try to talk to him on your own yet."

His breath caught. "If I promise, will you forgive me for taking so long to tell you I believe you about everything?"

"Yes."

He crushed her in his arms. "Will you let me love you?" His voice throbbed with longing.

"Do you have to ask?"

"I don't deserve you, Janet. I don't deserve your forgiveness or your understanding."

"Please don't ever say that again," she begged. "Don't you know how much I love you?"

"Yes," he cried softly. "I do know, and I'm humbled by your love. I adore you," he declared fiercely before lowering his mouth to hers.

Once again, her response blotted out the world. It was always like that. The minute she touched him, he went up in smoke and took her with him.

* * *

Janet jumped out of her car and hurried through the parking lot of the Ritter Building where Wade had opened up his own suite of offices. She breezed past Luanne who was in Salt Lake temporarily to find and train a new secretary for him. Inside Wade's private office, she found him seated at a new desk going through some papers.

"Hi, darling!"

His dark head came up and she found herself the object of a leering appraisal. No one could do it better than Wade. It made her heart skip a beat every time.

"Well, well. If it isn't my blushing bride whom I expected to be at home fixing dinner for her lord and master."

"Oops! You must be talking about someone else's bride. Did you forget it's my night at the homeless shelter?"

"That's tonight?"

She nodded. "But I'll forgive you if you'll take all of us to a show."

One brow dipped ominously. "All of us?"

"That's right. Ezra, Michael and Kenneth. The Denton brothers. They've been at the shelter for over a month and haven't done anything fun. I thought we'd treat them to an outdoor movie with hot dogs and popcorn. What do you say? We'll go in my car. They've been begging to ride in the convertible."

He flashed her a glance on the decidedly lewd side. "How old are they?"

"Not as old as you're thinking."

He grinned. "My bride is getting much too smart for me."

"What a sweet compliment. I'll take it. Do you think you'll mind a double feature of action/adventure?"

"Double, huh?"

"Yes. You know you'll love it!"

"And if I don't?"

"Then I'll arrange for another show after we take the children back to the shelter."

His silvery eyes narrowed. "What kind?"

"That's for me to know and you to find out."

"Do you swear?"

"I always keep my promises."

"Tonight I'll make certain that you do."

"What shall we do about your car?"

"There's a security guard on duty, so I'll leave it here overnight. If you don't mind driving me to work in the morning, there's something I want to discuss with you on the way home tonight."

Her hand crept to her throat. "I had no idea. Why don't I put off taking the boys out tonight?"

He shook his head. "No. What you want to do for them is of vital importance. Our talk can wait until later."

A dark foreboding enveloped her. "This has to do with Ty, doesn't it?"

"Yes. Roman Lufka phoned, then came by the office earlier this afternoon. It was an enlightening conversation."

"Under the circumstances, we'll only stay for one show. I couldn't sit through more than that."

"All right. Let's go."

The next three hours were a revelation. Wade went out of his way to entertain the boys, all under the age of twelve. But her heart was really touched when he bought enough treats for the boys to take something back to the shelter for every child who couldn't come with them.

She'd always known he would make a wonderful father. Tonight she saw his humanitarian side. It made her fall in love with him all over again.

"I know you don't want to be thanked for what you did, but I'm going to do it anyway. Those boys don't know where their father is. He took off a few months ago and their mother has had a horrible struggle. Tonight you gave them the gift of your time and interest. It was wonderful...." Her voice trailed off as tears stung her eyes.

"Don't give me any credit," he said as they pulled out of the shelter parking lot and headed for home. "Your heart has always reached out to the unfortunate. You were doing it in high school. It was Janet Larson who headed the sub for Santa program, read books for the blind and worked with the handicapped at the hospital. I only went along to be near you."

"Really. Then how do you explain the building you bought and had renovated for the homeless in Denver?"

His glance left the road to look at her for a brief moment. "How did you hear about that?"

"Luanne. We talked on the phone the other day. She happened to mention it along with her praise of the best boss she's ever worked for."

"Don't be fooled. I'm using it as a tax write-off."

"*Wade*," she cried softly. "I love you."

With one hand on the steering wheel, he reached for

hers with the other and squeezed it hard.

She kissed the tips of his fingers before letting his hand go. "Now that we're alone, tell me what Roman had to say."

"He said it's too soon to tell if Ty's dangerous because he hasn't made any kind of a threat. What Roman wants us to do is attend the reunion on Saturday night and act perfectly natural. We're not to let on that we noticed he was at the wedding or that we received his gift."

"Did he suggest what we should answer if Ty asks why we didn't invite him to the wedding?"

Wade nodded. "I'm supposed to calmly say that because of our past history, I didn't think he would be comfortable attending."

"That's brilliant of Roman!" she burst out excitedly. "You'll be able to broach the subject without seeming obvious."

"He also warned me that we should stay together the entire night. If we don't give him an opportunity to talk to either of us alone, then we'll both be witnesses to anything he has to say. Depending on Ty's behavior, we should be able to discern if something doesn't seem right, and go from there."

She studied her husband's striking profile. "How do you feel about that?"

"Good. Provided he shows up."

"He'll be there. He was president of the school. It's a tradition that the old president preside over the reunion."

"We'll see," he murmured, sounding far away. "If

you'll reach in the right pocket of my suit jacket, you'll find something interesting in there."

Intrigued, she twisted around far enough to pull his jacket off the back seat and put it in her lap. When she found the pocket, her fingers came in contact with two metallic objects.

"What are these?"

"Mini tape recorders you can hide in your clothes. Roman wants us to wear them. If Ty should say things that sound bizarre or are off the wall, he wants to be able to analyze the tapes."

She peered at them closely. "Annabelle uses these all the time in her work."

"Roman showed me how to put them on. He says they're more powerful than they look." By now, he'd pulled the car into their garage with the aid of the remote on her sun visor.

Janet put the recording devices back in his pocket. "Thank heaven for Roman. I'm for anything that helps resolve this nightmare plaguing our lives!"

He pulled her toward him and kissed her thoroughly. "Amen."

The high school gym hadn't changed. Most everyone had.

Janet had already seen her closest friends at the wedding, so there weren't any surprises there. As for the hundreds of others attending the reunion, loads of them were thinner, others were heavier and some looked amazingly the same.

A few of the boys she'd once known were losing their hair or had already lost it. Many of the girls she'd sung with in choir were pregnant with baby number two or three.

At five months along, Annie looked radiant in her stunning black maternity dress with her adorable cap of dark red curls.

Rand and Wade were both so gorgeous and male, no female in the room could stop staring at them.

It was hard to believe there was a time during their junior year when Janet and Annie had voted themselves the two most likely of their class never to get married. Then Wade had entered Janet's world....

As the four of them walked around chatting with everyone, Janet was very much afraid she was wearing the same stupid grin as Annie. But when you knew your husbands were the focal point of everyone's conversations, you couldn't help but feel like you were going to burst with pride.

There was only one thing that could have made the moment absolutely blissful—if she'd been wearing a maternity dress like Annie.

Hopefully at the twenty-year reunion she could bring pictures of her children like everyone else had done, and brag about them.

All the tables had filled up, but so far Janet hadn't seen a sign of Ty at the head table. For Wade's sake, it was imperative he show up. Her husband couldn't wait any longer to confront him.

She dared a glance at him while he was talking football with one of the guys from their old team. To anyone else he acted happy to be here, relaxed. His superb acting performance could have fooled anyone except Janet, who noticed how his keen gaze darted around the room time and again looking for the man who had cost them ten years of happiness.

"Hey, you guys…" Libby Wallace, the secretary of their class, had been named master of ceremonies and had stepped up to the mike at the head table. "It's so good to see you again. We know how excited you are to be here tonight. The officers have been planning this reunion for a long time. Our first since graduation.

"If you'll take your seats, the food can be served. It's a long program, so we'll get it started while you eat. That way, you can plan to be home by around, oh… I don't know… three, maybe four in the morning. I hope you told your baby-sitters you might be out late."

Her comments brought a roar from the crowd and a lot of clapping.

Wade flashed Janet a private smile that made her insides quiver. "She hasn't changed a bit since high school."

"She was always outgoing. Fearless. That's why they chose her to plan the program, I'm sure."

"A few statistics," Libby called out as their salads were served. "Tonight, twelve hundred of you walked through the gym doors for this event. That's impressive!

"You may have noticed that our illustrious president, Ty Clark, isn't here." Lowering her voice in a confiding tone, she said, "His wife phoned to tell me he was in a little fender bender a few minutes ago, but he'll be here as soon as he can. No one is supposed to know. Okay?"

Laughter exploded in the gym, but Janet's heart plummeted. It would be the perfect excuse if he decided not to show up at all. Wade's smile had turned into a grimace. She couldn't look into his eyes for fear of what she'd see.

Annie's and Rand's expressions remained deadpan. They knew what it would do to Wade if Ty didn't come.

"Now for the fun stuff. We're going to run a slide show up on the wall. As each picture appears, stand up if you're here, and we'll give everybody an up-to-date profile where we can. If we get stuck and you know something we don't, raise your hand."

The long list of histories began in alphabetical order. Janet leaned toward Annie. "You'll be first."

They'd made it to the main course of their meal before everyone heard the name Annabelle Forrester announced. Flush-faced, she stood up, her hand tightly clutched in Rand's.

A quick glance at the head table revealed that Ty still hadn't come in the gym. By now, Janet was starting to feel sick to her stomach, but she had to put on a smile with every eye staring in their direction. Wade assumed a pleasant expression, but she knew it was killing him.

"Would you believe our Annie became a cop like her dad? And then she moved on to become a famous private investigator." Hearing this, the crowd began to buzz with excitement.

"We all know what she did in Arizona. She went gunning for the state's most eligible bachelor, Rand Dunbarton of Dunbarton Electronics. Trust Annie to pull off the coup of the year and win *Today's Fortune* man of the year. Now they're married and going to have a baby."

Rand chuckled while his wife went all shades of red before sitting down. Wade reached across Janet to squeeze Annie's hand. When he removed it, Janet caught his somber gaze. She also caught something else out of the corner of her eye.

"He just came in," she mouthed to her husband.

Wade's head swerved in the direction of the head table. She shivered in apprehension as she watched Wade's eyes narrow on Ty and the blond woman with him.

Unable to eat another bite, she toyed with her food and tried to act like the world wasn't reeling on its axis.

More alums were introduced. Then suddenly Wade's graduation picture was projected on the wall. He looked so young and handsome, but most of all so *happy*. She had to swallow the sob that rose in her throat.

"Now talk about Mr. Heartbreak himself. Wade Holt. Champion debater, all-state linebacker, academic honor roll. He may be from Colorado, but we claim him. Today he's Mr. Rocky Mountain Enterprises, which I would say makes him the most illustrious man in our class."

As Wade rose reluctantly to his feet, the room exploded with clapping and whistles. He was given a standing ovation while Janet beamed at him.

You deserve this moment, my love. Every accolade.

Her gaze zeroed in on the one man in the room not celebrating. *You deserve this moment, too, Ty Clark.*

"We're going to change the order of things for a minute here. The reason being that Mr. Heartbreak himself married none other than our school's own Miss America, Janet Larson. Some of you may not know she graduated with honors from Stanford and is now with the prestigious law firm of Nebeker, Rowe, Brands and Larson.

"Stand up, Janet, while we flash a picture of your

wedding for everyone to see. They made a gorgeous couple ten years ago, and they make a gorgeous couple now!''

More clapping and shouts ensued along with wolf whistles from a bunch of guys in the room. Wade's sensuous smile caused her pulse to race before he slid a possessive arm around her shoulders and crushed her against his side.

''Libby overdid it,'' he whispered against her cheek after they'd sat down again, ''but I can't say I'm sorry.''

''Neither can I,'' she whispered back. ''You're my man. Now everybody knows it.''

She felt a strong, masculine hand slide up her thigh covered by the material of the royal-blue silk suit. She'd bought it especially to show off her wedding pin. But right now, it wasn't the pin or Ty she was thinking about. With Wade's hand on her leg throughout dessert and the rest of the introductions, she'd become a trembling mass of desire.

''That's all, folks. Hope you enjoyed the show. Now we'll hear a parting message from our president, Tyson Clark. While he comes up to the podium, we'll ask our treasurer, Matt Wirthlin, to lead us in the school song.''

Most everyone joined in except Wade, whose narrowed gaze studied Ty's progress to the mike. Janet covered her husband's hand with her own and left it there.

''Hi, guys. This has been a terrific night. But I think we've had enough program, don't you? It's time to mingle! Before we do however, I just want to say it's great to see all of you again. You're the greatest!'' Ty waved his hands over his head while everyone clapped. Then she heard the scrape of chairs as people began to socialize.

For the next twenty minutes the four of them were besieged by old friends. Wade kept his arm around Janet's waist. When Ty suddenly appeared in the crush without his wife, Janet was thankful for her husband's physical support.

She stared into Ty's smiling brown eyes, shocked that this benign-looking, dark blond man could have done anything as awful and cruel as he'd done to them without ever demonstrating one modicum of remorse.

"Janet and Wade." A fulsome smile wreathed his face. He nodded to them with his hands in the pockets of his khaki suit jacket. "Congratulations on your wedding. Because of a work problem, I arrived late at the ceremony, then had to slip out again without being able to offer my best wishes."

Wade's hand bit into her side. Neither of them had expected Ty to admit he had crashed their wedding. His temerity was nothing short of astounding. She feared her husband would challenge him right there. Instead, he nodded back. "You look exactly the same as the last time I saw you."

Oh, Wade. You're never going to get a confession out of him. I can understand why you believed him the first time. He's been terrifyingly manipulative for years, a past master at it.

"Well, I'll take that as a compliment. Janet, you're more beautiful than ever."

"Thank you," she replied, wondering how much longer she would be able to keep up this pretense before she started screaming. Under the circumstances, Wade was displaying incredible restraint. "Where's your wife? I was hoping to meet her."

"Oh, she's around here someplace catching up on gossip."

"I understand you're a mortician now."

Ty's smile didn't change, but Wade's remark caused his eyes to flicker. "That's right. We have two mortuaries in Salt Lake and we're building two more in Ogden and Provo."

"It sounds as if business is thriving."

"Not on the scale of Rocky Mountain Enterprises, but I'm not complaining."

Could anyone be smoother than Ty? Tragically he'd been bequeathed a politician's demeanor but none of the redeeming attributes that had gotten his father elected time after time.

How was Ty able to stand there and face them knowing what he'd done to them? His cold, meaningless smile was as chilling as that ghastly white seagull hidden in the box. She wanted to get out of the gym as fast as possible, but she could tell Wade wasn't about to go anywhere.

"Some of the guys at the frat house told me you've settled in Salt Lake."

"That's right. I always did love the skiing here better than in Colorado. Sounds like you still hang around the house a lot just like you used to do."

A strange laugh escaped Ty. Wade was beginning to rattle him.

Janet's legs started to shake. Her husband must have felt it because his arm tightened against her body.

"You're probably right. Do you have a problem with that?"

"Not me. I've got my wife. Since you knew Janet long before I did, I guess no one could understand better than you why I don't need or want anyone else."

Expecting a violent reaction of some kind, Janet couldn't believe it when Ty said, "Didn't I hear you were married before?"

"You heard correctly. As a matter of fact, I was told the same thing about you. Fortunately for me, I got it right the second time around. Didn't I, sweetheart."

Careful, darling, her heart cried as Wade brushed her lips with his own.

"No wedding ring, Janet?"

Furious because Ty had gone for the jugular, she had to retaliate in her own way. "I fell in love with Wade the first day he walked in our debate class. You remember my telling you about that, don't you, Ty? But there's something that only Wade knew about me. I'm allergic to metal and have never been able to wear jewelry. That's why on our wedding day he gave me this gorgeous diamond-and-sapphire pin in lieu of a ring. Isn't it exquisite?"

Ty stared at it for a moment. She watched his features harden. "You've done well for yourself, Wade. How does it feel to be able to buy anything now?"

Janet averted her eyes.

"When you've made your first million, then you'll be able to answer that question yourself. Now if you'll excuse us, we have a date with each other tonight. Ready, darling?"

CHAPTER EIGHT

WADE kissed the back of his wife's neck. "Janet? Are you awake?"

She made a sound but didn't turn over.

He frowned. For a while now—in fact, since the reunion over a week ago—she had become less and less responsive.

At first he'd presumed she was coming down with a cold, but he'd seen no symptoms. Last night they'd made love, but the same intensity wasn't there on her part.

There were even moments when he feared she might be tolerating him rather than joining him as an equally excited participant.

This morning he had awakened hungry for her. Where had the woman gone who used to reach eagerly for him in the early dawn?

When she'd told him that seeing Ty at the reunion had made her physically ill, he was beginning to wonder if the situation wasn't distressing her psychologically, as well.

Wade had put the microtapes in Roman's hands. Unfortunately the best P.I. in the business could find nothing key on them that had sent up a red flag. Ty Clark displayed signs of stifled anger. Certain comments had triggered his temper. But all of it seemed contained within what one could consider the limits of normal human response.

The fact that they knew Ty wasn't normal made the possibility of his being dangerous that much more difficult to determine. Unless he did something else overt or threatening, Roman didn't have enough to render a judgment.

Janet didn't seem to want to talk about it anymore. Wade couldn't blame her. He felt the same way. But if she was suppressing some deep seated fears, it could account for her behavior now.

After opening Ty's wedding present, it was possible she'd become so frightened of more unpleasant surprises that fear had started to immobilize her. He had to do something to allay it.

Without hesitation, he slid out of bed, threw on a robe and headed for the kitchen. It was his turn to fix her breakfast. Now that she'd become a housewife, the job she insisted she coveted most, she'd been waiting on him hand and foot. The time was long overdue to start showing her what she meant to him. Otherwise there might come a morning when he would wake up by her side and discover he'd killed their love.

That would kill *him*.

"French toast and grapefruit coming up."

Janet buried her face in the pillow to stifle her moan. She'd been lying there for the last little while plagued by a weakness that left her body in a cold sweat. Every so often a wave of nausea swept over her. The mere thought of food had become repellent.

Since the morning after the reunion, she'd slept a lot more and had noticed a decrease in her appetite. The few times she'd dropped by her mom's after doing some errands for the house, she'd turned down any offers of food.

Last night she'd felt sick but hadn't wanted to refuse Wade when he'd pulled her into his arms to make love. She'd tried hard to pretend she was enjoying every second of it, yet he had to sense that something was wrong.

In the middle of the night, a blinding headache had driven her from the bed while he slept. She'd searched the cabinet for some pain medicine. When she couldn't find it, she remembered the little bag she'd taken on their honeymoon. She thought there might still be something in there.

When she opened it, there was no painkiller. Instead, she discovered the vial of pills the doctor had prescribed for their trip to Africa. It was only half-empty!

She should have taken every tablet by now. Suddenly her illness made horrifying sense. Somehow she crept back to their bed. In agony she lay there for the rest of the night until exhaustion had taken over.

If she asked Wade to take away the food after he'd gone to all the trouble to prepare it, he would want to talk about her sickness. That's what frightened her.

Making a supreme effort, she turned on her back and sat up against the pillow. Sick as she felt, the sight of her husband's powerful frame covered only by a robe stirred her senses. This morning she could see no shadows in those crystalline gray eyes. They wandered over her face and body with an intensity that bordered on anxiety.

As he sank onto the side of the bed next to her with the tray, the smell of the French toast increased her nausea. To her chagrin, the talk she'd hoped to put off was inevitable now.

"Darling," she whispered. "I love you for going to all that effort, but I'm too sick to eat."

"You're so pale," he muttered in alarm. Without having to be asked, he left the room. When he came back seconds later, he was minus the tray. After taking his place beside her once more, he smoothed a hand over her forehead with the most infinite tenderness. "You feel cool, but your skin is clammy."

Hot tears trickled out of her eyes and down her cheeks. "I know what's wrong with me. It's my own fault that I'm sick."

With those words, her husband's expression underwent a drastic change. If ever a man looked in agony, he did. A mist covered his eyes.

"No, darling," he grated. "The fault lies with me. Always me. But God help me, no more."

She moved her head from side to side. "You mustn't take the blame for anything. Over and over again you warned me, but I was so happy we were back together, and then all the business about Ty I just—" She broke off talking, afraid she was going to be sick right in front of him.

"You need help getting up."

Like quicksilver, he picked her up as if she were so much fluff and carried her to the bathroom. By the time they reached the toilet, she'd begun to wretch, but they were dry heaves because there was nothing in her stomach to give up.

When he finally lowered her to the floor, she stood there shaking while she clung to him. "You'd better call

Dr. Frost, my internist. Tell him I think I've come down with malaria. Ask him what I should do.''

His gasp filled the room. "*Malaria*...?''

"Yes. I forgot to take the rest of the pills.''

"Good grief.''

Before she knew what was happening, he'd carried her back to the bed once more and was on the phone to her doctor. She lay there in a sick stupor waiting for the verdict.

"He hasn't arrived at his office yet. The nurse says you should go to Emergency. They'll phone him when they know something.''

"I don't want to go to the hospital.''

"I don't blame you, but this is your life we're talking about!'' The cords stood out in his neck. "*Dear God—* if anything were to happen to you...'' His voice shook with the kind of emotion she'd never heard come out of him before.

Within minutes, he'd dressed her and himself and had settled her in the Saab for the drive down the canyon.

When she saw the frantic look on his face, she felt so guilty. "I'm sorry, darling.''

"What in heaven's name do you have to be sorry about?'' he ground out.

"Because I told you not to worry about my taking the pills. I remember saying something about the fact that I was a woman who'd been looking after herself for a long time. I guess I was trying so hard to compete with Claire that I—''

"*Claire?*'' His incredulity was a hundred percent genuine.

"Yes. You told me she was a wonderful person. I knew she had to be or you would never have married her. I've been afraid that I might not measure up."

He expelled an oath she couldn't decipher. "Claire was one of the secretaries I inherited when I took over my first business out of college and made a success out of it. We became friends. When her mother died, she naturally turned to me for comfort.

"I needed someone who needed me, and I got tired of going home to an empty apartment night after night. I learned to love many things about her. We eventually talked of marriage and children. I warned her I wasn't very good husband material, but she said she was willing to take the risk.

"Claire didn't have her heart set on a church wedding. That was a relief to me because I was pretty sure I couldn't step inside a church after our broken engagement with all its ramifications. So we were married by a civil servant at the county courthouse.

"Trust me, Janet. If ever anyone struggled in vain to live up to someone else, it was Claire who I fear was in constant competition with you. She knew about you. After she'd suffered her miscarriage, she told me her feelings for me had changed. Until she brought up the subject of divorce, I never realized that she felt threatened by your memory."

"Oh, Wade—"

"Don't you dare say you're sorry!" he bit out. "Our marriage was wrong. I did love her in my own way, but I obviously wasn't *in* love with her. A divorce freed us to get on with our lives."

"A fine wife you've got now," Janet moaned as another attack of nausea left a film of moisture on her skin. "If I hadn't behaved like a silly child, none of this would have happened."

"I have no complaints. Do you understand me?"

She'd learned to tell the difference between his display of real anger and the kind that masked anxiety. Right now, he was more than a little worried about her physical well-being.

He pulled the car to the doors of the emergency entrance of University Hospital too fast and was forced to use his brakes. She lay there listless against the seat while an attendant brought her a wheelchair. Once Wade had helped her into it, he told the attendant he'd be right back to sign her in.

This would be Janet's first visit to a hospital as a patient. But she felt too sick to be frightened. The attendant wheeled her into a cubicle and helped her on with a hospital gown. Once she'd stretched out on the bed, he drew the sheet to her neck.

"Here's a pan in case you feel sick again."

He disappeared. It wasn't long before a nurse came in to take her vital signs. When she went out, Wade came in.

"Come close to me," she begged.

He pulled up a chair next to her and grasped one of her hands. For a moment, he didn't say anything, just pressed it to his cheek and kissed her wrist.

Wade had always been loving with her, but today she sensed a change in him. A deeper tenderness and affection. Like the way he'd been while they were dating in high school and college, when his emotions had been more open.

And more vulnerable to pain.

"Do you want me to phone your mother?"

"No, darling, but thank you for offering. I—I'd rather be told how bad my malaria is first. When I find out what I have to do to get better, then I'll tell them."

"That's probably for the best," he murmured. "You're their only child. This is going to come as a shock to them. All these years they've raised and protected you. Then I haul you off to deepest Africa and bring you back ill."

"I knew you were going to say that," she said in a quivering voice.

"My presence in your life has caused you nothing but grief."

"How can you say th—"

"Hi... Mr. and Mrs. Holt? I'm Dr. Murray."

Wade rose to his full height and shook the doctor's hand.

The young-looking physician eyed her directly. "What makes you think you've got malaria?"

"I—I forgot to take all my antimalarial pills while we were on our honeymoon in Kenya."

"What are your symptoms? When did they start?"

He wrote her responses on his clipboard.

"I tell you what. I'm going to examine you, and we'll get some blood work done. It shouldn't be too long before we know exactly what's wrong with you."

"Can my husband stay?"

"I only need a few minutes alone with you."

"I'll be right outside the curtain." Wade brushed her

mouth with his lips before he disappeared from the cubicle.

"I don't know what's wrong with me," she admitted to the doctor. "I feel like a frightened little child."

"You feel sick, that's why. Not everyone comes in here thinking they have malaria." He smiled. "I doubt you have it."

She blinked. "You do?"

"You haven't mentioned fever. That's one of the symptoms. From everything you've described to me, it doesn't sound like malaria. But knowing you've recently come back from Africa and that you didn't take all your medicine, we'll make certain."

In very little time he completed the examination.

"If I don't have malaria, what do you think is wrong with me?"

"I'm not sure. It could be several things, even a bad strain of flu you picked up overseas. Someone will be in from the lab shortly to draw blood and get a urine sample. Then we'll know more. I'll tell your husband he can join you now."

Wade took longer than she thought he would to come back in. When he reappeared, he seemed to be a little less tense. "Did the doctor tell you it might not be malaria?"

"Yes," he said emotionally, grasping her hand again. "Let's pray he's right. What can I do for you?"

"Make the nausea go away?" She managed to give him a half smile.

His solemn eyes searched hers relentlessly. "Janet... I—"

"Hello!" the lab technician announced his presence.

"This will only take a minute. Here's a cup with your name on it. Go to the rest room around the corner after I'm through. Just leave it on the shelf and I'll get it."

By the time all the testing had been done, Janet was too nauseous and enervated to keep her eyes open. She curled on her side toward her husband and clung to his strong, warm hand. "Promise you won't leave if I go to sleep?"

"As if I would," he returned in a husky voice.

"Annie? It's Wade."

"I'm glad you phoned. I've been trying to reach Janet for the past couple of days, but she hasn't returned any of my calls."

"She hasn't been well. In fact, we're at University Hospital's E.R. right now trying to find out what's wrong."

"You're kidding!"

"I wish I were," he said in a shaky voice. "A few minutes ago she fell asleep, thank heaven. I decided this would be the best time to call you."

"You don't sound that great yourself."

He closed his eyes. "I'm not. Listen, Annie when all is said and done, I'm afraid I may be Janet's problem."

"What do you mean?"

His breath caught. "You don't have to pretend with me. We both know what I've done to her," he said in thick tones.

Total quiet reigned for a few minutes.

"Can I ask you a question, Wade?"

"Of course."

"This is truth time now. Remember it's Annie you're talking to, and I loved her long before you did."

"I know."

"Before Ty ruined everything, did you ever, even for one millisecond, detect a dishonest bone in her body?"

His head went back so he was looking at the ceiling. "No."

"I'm glad you said that because she doesn't have one. She never will."

He gripped his cell phone more tightly. "You can choose to believe me or not, but I came to that conclusion on our honeymoon. Unfortunately I didn't make it clear to Janet until the night we opened Ty's present."

There was another moment of quiet, then he heard Annie expel a long, shuddering sigh of relief. "Oh, Wade. I don't know all the reasons why it took you so long to figure it out. The only point that matters is, you did!"

He swallowed hard. "Except that all the stress has probably made her ill." The whole time he'd been talking in hushed tones on his phone, he'd stood at the far end of the cubicle with his back to Janet so she couldn't hear him.

"What if something happens to her, Annie?" he said with tears in his voice. "What if I nev—" Emotion choked off the rest of his words.

"I'll be right there, Wade."

He heard her click off.

Doing the same, he put the phone back in his pocket. As he turned to his wife, terror seized his heart.

She lay in the same position as before with her eyes closed. The skin of her face held a faintly greenish cast.

Even her lips. He'd never seen anyone lose color like that before, except—

"My wife!" he shouted as he raced for the front desk. "Someone help her! Quick!"

One of the nurses ran to the cubicle with Wade on her heels. She started taking vital signs. Wade was beside himself until Janet's eyelids fluttered open for a moment, then closed again.

"How do you feel, Mrs. Holt?"

"Horribly nauseated."

"Hang on for a few more minutes."

"Wade?" Janet called out in a weak voice.

"I'm here, darling."

"That's good."

Frantic with worry, he walked to the opening of the cubicle with the nurse. "Can't you do anything for her?"

"Not until the doctor knows the results of the tests."

"She's green."

"A lot of people go that color when they're nauseated. I know it's alarming to you, but it's really quite common." She patted his arm. "Your wife's not dying. She's not even close. I think maybe you're the one who needs to sit down for a while."

With the scare over for the moment, Wade's steps were lethargic as he went back to the cubicle and sank onto the chair beside his wife. When the doctor came in a few minutes later, Wade didn't notice because his head was buried in his hands.

"Mr. Holt?"

He jumped to his feet. "*Thank God* you're back. Do you know what's wrong with my wife?"

He smiled. "I do. Let's tell your wife, too, shall we?" The doctor moved next to Janet. "Mrs. Holt?"

She opened her eyes. "Yes?" she responded sluggishly.

"You don't have malaria or anything like it. May I be the first to congratulate you and your husband. The test came back positive. You're pregnant!"

Wade thought he was going to faint.

"I'm going to have a baby?" Her voice came out like a happy little squeal.

"No doubt about it."

"Is this morning sickness?"

"I'm afraid so. You've got a pretty bad case of it, but there are some wonderful drugs on the market to relieve it. Do you have an obstetrician?"

"Yes." Wade spoke for her and gave the doctor her obstetrician's name. Wade was so giddy with joy he could hardly contain his euphoria.

"Good. I'll put through a call to him now and see what he would prescribe. We'll be giving her an IV to hydrate her. Depending on what he says, she'll probably be able to go home in a few hours. Even with the drug, don't expect instant results. It may take forty-eight hours before she starts to feel more like herself."

"Doctor?" she murmured.

"Yes?"

"Do you think pregnant hippos and giraffes get sick like this, too?"

Wade burst into laughter. The doctor joined in. They both had to wipe their eyes. Finally the doctor said, "I'm sure I don't know, Mrs. Holt, but I would imagine they do."

She closed her eyes. "All I can say is, the poor things." The last came out as a groan.

Laughter erupted again.

As Wade accompanied the doctor from the cubicle, he caught sight of Annie rushing toward him. When she drew close, he caught her in his arms and twirled her around.

"Annie, Annie, we're going to have a baby!"

"Oh, my gosh. That means our children will only be five months apart! Maybe they'll end up being best friends, too."

"I'm counting on it."

"I've got to phone Rand!"

"You do that."

In full view of everyone in the E.R., he gave her a kiss of happiness before lowering her to the floor.

Six days later, Janet was able to stand in front of the bathroom mirror without wanting to heave.

"I don't look quite as green around the gills this morning, Mom," she said into the cordless phone. "Poor Wade thinks he has to put up with nine months of this. Tonight I'm going to surprise him. Tell Dad I'm doing much better, and we'll see both of you tomorrow. Love you."

She turned off the phone, then stepped into the shower, excited for tonight to come. Wade hadn't had a wife in the true sense of the word for over two weeks. But that was all going to change when he walked through the door at six.

She'd wanted to die of joy after the doctor told her she was expecting a baby. But the miraculous news hadn't come without strings.

Never again in her life would she pass off another woman's morning sickness as nothing more than a minor inconvenience for such a great blessing. The truth was, for the first two days after coming home from the hospital, she'd felt like she was dying. Wade had refused to go to work. But after she got past that hump, she convinced him she was going to be all right.

The first day away from her he phoned constantly. She finally had to tell him to stop or there was no point in his going to the office at all.

Wade's mom had called several times when he wasn't home, overjoyed by the news. She wanted to know how Janet was feeling and confided that she'd been horribly sick carrying one of Wade's sisters.

His mother was a nurse and had some good, practical advice for her. It all helped. Janet didn't even want to think about what women had done before the advent of modern drugs.

Annie phoned once a day to talk, but she couldn't relate because she'd never suffered from the problem. She had another kind. Not enough room for the baby who the doctor said looked like a whopper. Annie's greatest fear at the moment was delivering a twelve-pound, twenty-three inch girl. History's first offensive linewoman for the Green Bay Packers, her favorite pro football team.

Janet laughed till she cried.

In fact, she laughed in spurts all day long as she prepared a surprise dinner for Wade. He'd worked like a

Trojan unpacking boxes after the moving van had arrived with her things. She found her favorite blue-and-white-striped tablecloth to set the round table out on the deck.

Wade loved sirloin steak. She'd marinated several and would throw them on the grill when she heard his car pull into the garage.

The phone rang just as she finished decorating a chocolate cake, his favorite kind. On top of the frosting she'd used chocolate chips to spell the word "Daddy".

"Hello?"

"Hi! Is this Janet?"

"Yes. Who's this?" The caller ID said "unavailable" on it.

"It's Art Wood."

"Oh, yes, Art. How are you?"

"I'm great. How was the honeymoon?"

"Fantastic."

"That's good. I wondered if your hubby was around. Lex and Ty want to get together for handball next week. If Wade came, we'd have a foursome."

Her heart missed a beat. Had Ty put Lex up to this?

"Well, it sounds fun, but I can't speak for Wade. If you'll give me your number, I'll have him call you back."

"Sure."

After the call ended, her hand stayed frozen to the receiver.

"No!" she said out loud to the kitchen. *"I'm not going to let this ruin our special night."*

She slipped the note with the phone number in the nearest drawer, then proceeded to forget about it because the garage door had started to open. Quickly she hurried out to the grill with the steaks, then took the chilled white wine from the refrigerator and poured it into a tall-stemmed crystal glass.

Carefully so she wouldn't spill, she carried it to the top of the stairs and waited for him.

Wade was hurrying so fast he took the steps two at a time. Luckily she moved out of the way to avoid a collision.

"Janet!"

She'd surprised him all right. He stood there out of breath in the tan suit he'd worn to work. His beautiful gray eyes swept over her in blatant male admiration.

The project to make herself as attractive as possible in a summer print dress had paid off. She could feel his excitement as his mind began to register the obvious. She was back to her old self, with one fundamental difference.

"For you, my lord and master." She put the glass to his lips. "Drink, and forget thy troubles."

As if in a trance, he emptied half of it, then set it on the hall credenza.

"I would join you, but since you've made me pregnant with your child, I'm afraid I must abstain. From alcohol, that is.

"Of course," she said in her most seductive voice, "there are other pleasures I don't have to abstain from. Indeed, I find that my condition has made me look forward to them with even more anticipation than is deemed proper, for a proper wife, that is. But I find I don't wish to be a proper wife. Not tonight," she said in a voice trembling with longing.

She heard her name cried before his mouth fell upon hers and she was crushed against his powerful body. Filled with the greatest happiness she'd ever known, she gave herself up to this magnificent husband who was kissing her, thrilling her, transporting her to their own private world of rapture.

"The steaks burned!"

Wade caught her hand across the deck table. "After the feast you served me in our bedroom, do you think I would even notice?"

A faint blush crept up her cheeks. He couldn't stop staring at her. After the scare she'd given him at the hospital, this was like having his gorgeous wife back in Technicolor.

"Do you know how good it is to see you eating anything, let alone potatoes and salad?"

She gave him the benefit of her full-bodied smile. "It all tastes good. The medicine has finally kicked in. I feel like a new person."

"Just don't overdo it," he growled playfully.

"Except with you."

His smile faded. "Except with me."

The background music from the stereo, the love light in her eyes transformed him until he didn't know himself.

"I have another surprise for you. Stay there and I'll get it."

He lounged back in the chair, content to watch her movements as she drifted into the kitchen. That beautiful body held his child. He'd been granted two miracles and would guard them both with his life.

Though Claire's doctor had assured Wade that there was nothing they could have done to prevent her miscarriage, Wade had carried around a residue of guilt that if he'd loved her enough, it might not have happened.

Janet would have such a surfeit of love that their baby would enter this world healthy and perfect. Then their dream for a family would be realized.

Daddy. A grin of delight crossed his face as she set the cake in front of him. He tasted the frosting with his finger. "You're spoiling me rotten, Mrs. Holt."

"That's the idea. Except that I forgot the knife to cut it."

"I'll get it. You've done enough for one night." He forced her to sit down, then gave her a hard kiss on the mouth. "I'll be right back."

One of the drawers held the silverware. The trick was to remember where he'd put everything. On the third try he found a knife. He also discovered a piece of paper with a number written in Janet's hand.

He carried both to the table. After they'd finished the last of the delicious dessert, he showed her the paper.

"This phone number was in the drawer. Is it important?"

Not by a flick of her lashes did her body English change. But a certain stillness emanating from her alerted him that something was wrong. "Could we talk about it tomorrow?" came the imploring voice.

Her black hair glistened in the candlelight. Those brilliant blue eyes shone like the sapphire in the pin she had fastened to her dress. Being this near to her made him breathless all over again to possess her.

Now was the time to prove to her that he was a changed man.

"We don't ever have to talk about it. Are you up to a dance with me, Mrs. Holt? It's a beautiful night. I want to hold you in my arms beneath all these stars."

The way she ran from her chair to meet him halfway was his reward. She was the perfect height for him. Her voluptuous curves and long legs fitted the whipcord length of his body as if they'd been designed to interlock.

"Have you been thinking of names for our baby?"

"Constantly," she admitted.

"So have I."

"Do you like the idea of knowing ahead of time whether it will be a boy or a girl?"

"Honestly?"

"If you had to ask that question, then your answer is no." She pressed her lips to his jaw. "I want to be surprised, too."

He caught her mouth with his own in a long, passionate kiss. "I figure that if the parent hippos and giraffes have to wait to know the outcome, then who are we to be any different?"

"Oh, Wade…" Her eyes brimmed with unshed tears. "I love you so much and I'm so happy about the baby. Won't it be exciting to tell our son or daughter one day, when they start to ask about those things, that they were conceived on safari in Africa?"

Wade started to chuckle. He never knew what was going to come out of his precious wife. "So you're planning to give away all our secrets?"

"Just the obvious one."

He pulled her tighter against him. "What color shall we paint the nursery?"

"It's off-white right now. Maybe we could put up one of those children's border prints next to the ceiling."

"I'm sure there's one we could find with an animal motif."

"That would be perfect!" She threw her arms around his neck and hugged him.

Intoxicated by the starry night and the woman in his arms, he slow danced with her for a while. Ten years' separation had taught him to savor every moment.

"Darling?" Her chest rose and fell.

"Don't talk. Don't break the spell."

"I—I have to. It's about that note. Art Wood phoned. He and Lex want to get up a foursome to play handball."

"With Ty making up the fourth person?"

Wade could read her mind. "Yes." Her voice shook. "Roman said he wanted to know if Ty did anything else."

He kissed the side of her neck. "Don't worry. I'll inform him first thing in the morning. I'll also call Lex and tell him I won't be free to do anything for an indefinite period. Being a newlywed and a father-to-be is taking all of my time."

Her body gave a little quiver. "I'm so glad you said that. I'm afraid of him."

"Don't be. He can't hurt us anymore."

"I think you're wrong. Something tells me he's dangerous and might hurt you." She'd stopped dancing and pulled a little way apart from him to look into his eyes.

"Sweetheart we don't have to worry with all our good friends working on the case."

One tear, then another, trickled down her cheeks. "You don't know how much I want to believe that. I love you so much."

Humbled by her sweetness, he buried his face in her hair. "My wonderful, beautiful, constant wife."

She rubbed the back of his head with her hand. "Knowing what I now know about your parents' marital problems, combined with the things Ty said to you to destroy you on such a deeply personal level, I marvel that you survived it. Ty mustn't be allowed to do anything else to hurt us.

"Roman backs Annie's assessment of Ty. For some nefarious reason of his own, it's *you* Ty has targeted. This invitation to play handball was orchestrated by him. He can't seem to let you alone."

Wade finally raised his head. "I agree. Do you feel comfortable about following Roman's advice in this, whatever it is?"

"Yes. He's the best at what he does."

"Then so be it. Now I think it's time we locked up and went to bed. I know a mother-to-be who's knocked herself out today. It's time to take care of her."

CHAPTER NINE

"THAT'S everything off the van, Mrs. Holt. If you'll sign here."

Janet had been directing traffic as they brought in a brown leather sofa, an oak rolltop desk, the box springs and mattress of a double bed, sporting equipment, Wade's computer and everything to go with it.

She couldn't wait for the men to leave so she could start unpacking the boxes containing Wade's clothes and personal items. After signing her name at the bottom of the paper, she walked the movers to the front door.

The second they left, she hurried to the bedroom to undo the wardrobe and box. Naturally she didn't recognize any of his clothes. Ten years had gone by. It was silly to feel a letdown because everything was unfamiliar. Now was not the time to think about Claire's contribution to any of his things.

Wade had put the past to rest. She should do nothing less. But much later in the afternoon, while she was opening the last box, she came across a sealed brown envelope. Her first instinct was to undo the flap, but her hands hesitated.

This was private. This was all he had left of a marriage with Claire no matter how short-lived. They'd loved each other enough to marry. She'd been there for him when Janet couldn't be. There had been love and affection. Claire had carried his child and lost it. They'd had a history together.

Janet had begged Wade to forget Ty. Now she needed to take her own advice and let Claire go. Slowly she walked over to their dresser and placed the envelope in the bottom drawer beneath the sweaters she'd folded there.

When she stood up, she was so surprised to see Wade standing in the doorway she let out a small gasp. "I didn't know you were home."

"I parked in front of the garage. Obviously you were deep in thought and didn't hear me come in."

"The van arrived this morning. I—I've been putting your things away."

"So I see. As far as I can tell, you didn't leave anything for me to do. You're working much too hard for your condition."

"I feel fine."

She could feel his penetrating gaze. "You could have opened the envelope. We have no secrets."

So he *had* seen her put it in the drawer.

"I didn't want to invade your privacy."

"Then we'll do it together because I don't know what's in there. My mother handed it to me while I was getting everything ready for the packers to come."

Her head was bowed. "I thought—"

"I know what you thought. The mementos of my marriage to Claire are in safekeeping at my parents' home. She was their first daughter-in-law and they loved her as much as I did."

After those words of explanation, Janet sank onto the edge of the bed without saying anything. Wade stepped past her and retrieved the fat envelope from the drawer. The mattress gave beside her before he slit open the top and reached inside.

Janet let out a cry when he pulled out all the letters she'd sent him in Denver. They spilled onto the floor. One for every day of those five nightmarish weeks. None of them had been opened.

"I told her to throw them away," he whispered in anguish. "This had to be my mother's last effort to make me believe you, darling. She always believed in you. When I went back to Denver, she knew you were my life!" The tears in his voice were a revelation.

"I've always loved your mother because she was your mother. Now I love her for herself because I know the goodness of her heart." Quietly Janet slipped off the bed and knelt to put the letters back in the envelope. She lifted her head to her husband. "I'm going to call her tonight and tell her."

He sucked in his breath. "Let's call her now and tell her together."

"Oh, Wade..." She wrapped her arms around his legs. Another prayer had just been answered. "It will make her so happy to know you've forgiven her."

He nodded before she handed him the phone.

The next few minutes were emotional ones. There came a point when Janet left the room so Wade could talk to his mother in total privacy. This moment had been years in coming. There would be no more shadows in their lives now except one.

A half hour later, Wade came out on the deck to find her. He brought an air of peace with him.

"Umm. Steaks again?"

"You got cheated last night."

"You want to make a bet?" he whispered devilishly.

She smiled. "Sit down and I'll serve you."

He did her bidding.

"I met with Roman today," he volunteered before biting into his corn on the cob. "He told me to accept the invitation."

Janet had been wondering when the subject would come up again, but she cringed at the news. "What's his reasoning?"

"He's planning to set up a sting operation. However, no one's going to force you to do something you feel you can't handle. With the baby coming, I'm not taking any chances."

She frowned. "I would do anything for this to be over. The sooner the better. Once he's out of our lives for good, there won't be any more stress."

He squeezed her hand. "All right. Here's the scenario. Annie and Rand are going to plan a party at their house. They'll invite a bunch of our closest high school and college friends on the pretext that after seeing everyone at the reunion, Annie couldn't wait for another get-together.

"She'll arrange to have the invitations reach everyone the day after I play handball with Ty and the guys. For my part, I'm supposed to be congenial and friendly, and try not to push any of his buttons.

"Hopefully he'll be so livid because his riling didn't get him anyplace that he'll leap at the chance to attend a party where you and I are certain to be invited. There's the added incentive of being a guest in the home of the legendary Rand Dunbarton. It's right up Ty's alley."

"That's true. He's all show."

"Annie has a plan to expose him. I have no idea what it is. Depending on how he handles it, she'll proceed from there. Roman's going to be at the party in case of trouble."

"Good," she blurted with relief. "Ty's had it his own way long enough. But he's never come up against Roman's kind of expertise. While you finish your dinner, I'm going to call my friend and ask her what I can do to help."

He grabbed her hand and kissed it before she hurried inside to the phone.

Annabelle and Rand's house could have been plucked right out of a jasmine-scented hillside in Provence, France. On the one and only night Wade had seen the view of the city from their backyard, he'd been in such hell he couldn't have had any conception of its fabulous Mediterranean decor.

One side of the back patio held an herb garden. There was a terraced garden of lemon and orange trees below that. Bougainvillea and other flowering shrubs bordered the velvety lawn that swept down to the edge of their property.

Guests could mingle indoors or out and feel like they'd stepped on French soil for a night. Roman tended bar in a black-and-white outfit while uniformed maids circulated with the drinks. The alcohol flowed liberally, part of the plan because Ty could party with the best of them.

On the other side of the patio a live band played everything from French love songs to flamenco and the macarena. No one lucky enough to be invited to the Dunbartons' had a clue everything had been done to impress one guest. As if on cue, Ty made his appearance early in the evening with his wife and began making his rounds with the crowd in true politician style. According to Roman, he was now working on his fourth mai tai.

Wade and Janet had their orders to separate and mingle throughout the evening. Sooner or later, Ty would be more inclined to make a move if he could see each was without the other.

Lex and Art had come together with their wives. With drinks in hand, they converged on Wade, who'd been nursing the same ginger ale for over an hour. Tonight's effort demanded he be on full alert, but no one else knew he wasn't imbibing like the rest of them.

Out of the corner of his eyes Wade watched his wife in a flowing, full-length white evening gown. More radiant because of her pregnancy, she took his breath away as she moved from group to group, the cynosure of every eye. A ginger ale remained in her hand, as well. Every so often she glanced around her until she caught his eye, sending him a private message that said, "This is it."

He'd never quite understood the appeal of being a private investigator. But tonight, with the scene set and ready to be played out, everyone at their stations knowing exactly what they had to do and the adrenaline flowing, he felt a certain excitement at dicing with danger. He could swear his wife felt it, too.

Art rolled his eyes. "Did you get a load of one of the rooms on the main floor with all those Mexican and

South American artifacts? I mean, it's fantastic. Like a museum. I guess one of their hobbies is archaeology.''

"No, I didn't see it," Wade lied. "Where is it exactly?"

"We'll show you. Come on."

Wade followed the four of them into the house. As he passed through the patio doors, he noticed Ty watching their progress from the bar. Roman and Wade exchanged a private glance before he went on through to the hallway.

Both Annie and Rand shared a passion for ancient history whether it be Middle Eastern or Mesoamerican. Every aspect of their home could be photographed for *Architecture Digest*. No doubt the guests would be talking about this evening for a long time to come.

Lex whistled as he looked around. "How would it feel to bring in the kind of money this guy has?"

"Ask Wade." Art grinned. "He knows how it feels."

Wade smiled. "I've been lucky, but I'm not in Rand's class, believe me."

"We're going to go look at the nursery," one of their wives said.

When they had gone, Lex turned to Wade. "Hey... now that we're alone, do you mind if we ask you a question?"

"Go right ahead."

"Why do you let Ty take digs at you without ever saying anything back?"

A fresh punch of adrenaline hit his bloodstream. "What do you mean?"

"Come on, Wade. When we hung around the frat house, he was always at your throat. But the way he was on your case the other night, it seemed like he was out for blood. I was ready to knock his teeth in.''

Wade eyed them both squarely. ''Why do you guys pretend you don't know?''

Both frowns seemed genuine. Art spoke first. ''What are you talking about?''

''You mean you're going to stand there and tell me you don't know why I left the university and broke my engagement to Janet?''

Art shook his head in bewilderment. ''In the first place, it was none of our business. We figured it had to be something serious because I've never seen a couple more in love than the two of you.''

An expletive escaped Wade's lips. ''You two were at the house the day I came back from Denver and couldn't find Janet anywhere. You were the ones who told me to talk to Ty, that you'd seen her with him at the Canyon Inn and he would explain.''

''Yeah.'' They nodded.

Wade rubbed the back of his neck. ''Why are you acting so innocent when you knew exactly what Ty would tell me about him and Janet when he came to the frat house that night?''

Lex made a noise. ''You mean those lies about his sleeping with her while you were away? Nobody even listened. Wade...everybody knew he hated your guts because Janet was in love with you. He and half the guys in the fraternity would have loved to date Janet, but she never knew anyone else existed but you.''

''Ty always talked trash about you,'' Art added, ''but everybody liked you and knew he was jealous of you. The only reason he got into the fraternity was because his dad was governor. He's a loser. He doesn't have any friends. That's why he still hangs around the frat house. We play handball with him sometimes to be nice, but everybody knows the stuff that comes out of his mouth is pure fiction.''

Fiction? Wade reeled.

As comprehension dawned, both men's faces sobered. Art shook his head. ''Wade...you didn't believe him?'' He stared at Wade. ''You did! That's why you took off and never came back. Nobody could figure out what happened. Janet was never the same again. We heard she suffered a nervous breakdown.''

''He broke you two up deliberately!'' Lex uttered grimly. ''No wonder he was trying to wipe you all over the floor the other night. He couldn't handle knowing that you and Janet got back together anyway.''

Long before tonight, Wade had received confirmation that everything Ty had ever told him was a lie, but there was something about hearing it from the guys.... They had been his friends all along.

''I did believe him,'' he admitted quietly. ''The reasons why are no longer relevant. Thanks for being straight with me. Keep this conversation to yourselves, all right?''

''Is this a private party, or can anyone join in?'' Annie's voice interrupted them. ''I promised Ty a private tour of the house.''

Ty's eyes looked glazed over as he made it inside with another drink in hand. ''Annie's come a long way since our debating days, wouldn't you say, Wade?''

''I don't know. She was pretty spectacular back then, too. If Janet hadn't climbed into my heart the first day she walked into chemistry class, I'd have fallen for my favorite redhead on the spot."

Annie grinned. "Now he tells me. Lex and Art...I've been ordered to break up this scene. Your wives want a dance with you before the band plays its last number."

"I knew it." Lex groaned.

"Let's go," Art muttered. "Wade? We'll get together soon for some more handball."

"I'll call you guys next week."

When they left, Annie said, "This is almost like old times. All we're missing is Janet."

Ty's eyes surveyed the stunning room. "I'm surprised your wife isn't in here with you."

"That's funny. I was just thinking I'm *not* surprised *your* wife isn't in here with you."

"What's that supposed to mean?"

"Whatever you choose to think it means."

The other man took a swallow of his drink. "How did you like my wedding present?"

Bless you, Annie.

Too much alcohol had taken Ty off his guard. He'd forgotten about their hostess standing a few feet away.

"Even for you, it was rather plebeian. But since you weren't invited to the wedding, I suppose it's all we could have expected."

Ruddy color stained Ty's cheeks. "You'd better keep an eye on your wife tonight or—"

"Or what?" Wade preempted him. "Are you suggesting I might find her in some other man's bed before the evening is out?"

The plastic smile was in place. "It's a possibility."

"Well, at least we know it won't be yours."

Ty weaved on his feet, staring at his drink. "You never could handle that I made it with her first."

"Oh, give it up, Ty!" Annie broke in, still sounding friendly. "You sound like a broken record. That lie only worked with Wade once."

His head slowly turned toward her. It looked like he was having trouble focusing. "But it worked."

With a finesse only Annie possessed, she'd elicited the long-sought after confession. Wade could only marvel.

"Don't you think it's time you grew up and stopped making a total fool of yourself? Nothing *worked*! Wade and Janet are back together again, tighter than ever. They're going to have a baby."

The glass slipped from Ty's hands and splintered on the parquet flooring.

"If you go on harassing them, I'm going to have to slap a restraining order on you and haul you before a judge, bud. I would hate to do that because as I see it, I'm about the only friend you've got left who still cares about you."

His dark blond head reared back. "You—haul *me*?"

"That's right."

An angry laugh escaped him. "You wouldn't dare."

"Try me and find out. Do you really want your wife humiliated? Do you want your dad to be embarrassed by his secondborn son? He's high profile now. Rumor has it he plans to run for senator in a few years. This kind of copy will make it into every newspaper and media story across the country."

"Annie, you're awfully cute with that red hair and

curves all over the place. But you don't scare me with talk like that.''

Wade had to see what happened next to believe it.

Annie moved toward Ty and used some motion that flipped all 180 pounds of him flat on his back.

Ty let out a grunt. He stared up at her in a complete daze.

"You know something, bud? You look awfully stupid lying there. I'm booking you for defamation of character, purposeful alienation of affection, illegal loitering on church premises, mail harassment and intoxication.

"You're allowed one phone call from the jail. You'd better engage the best attorney money can buy you. I'll call your dad and tell him he can post bond until you appear before the judge.

"Roman? You can come in now.''

As if it was a scene from a movie, Wade watched in fascination as Annie's boss strolled into the room still dressed in his bartender outfit. Janet and Rand were right behind him.

His wife's brilliant blue eyes strained toward Wade's before she took a flying leap into his arms. He crushed her to him while Roman handcuffed Ty and read him his rights. The next few minutes were instructive as Roman picked Ty up from the floor and assisted him out of the room.

By now, Rand had wrapped his arms around his pregnant wife whose little mound had started to protrude. His big body shook with laughter. Wade couldn't hold back, either.

Annie looked sheepishly at Janet. "I kind of overdid it.''

Wade could hardly talk. "'Kind of' doesn't begin to cover it."

"Well, he got me going, and I couldn't stop."

"You know what they say about redheads," Rand quipped.

"Nothing except the intoxication part will stand up in court. I kind of made everything up as I went along, but he's so drunk he won't remember it when he wakes up in the morning surrounded by more drunks. It will be an experience for him that's been long overdue. One thing for sure. He'll know he's in real trouble if he ever so much as looks at the two of you again."

Wade relinquished his hold on his wife long enough to reach for Annie and give her a long hug. "You were sensational. Where did you learn to toss a man like that? The police academy?"

"Heavens no. I picked it up watching football."

The room collapsed with laughter before Rand and Annie went to find a broom and dustpan to clean up the glass.

Wade pulled Janet back into his arms. "Darling? Do you have any idea where Ty's wife is?"

She nodded. "Roman told Lex and Art there was a problem, so they drove her home. He's going to run by her house later."

"That's good. I'm glad she didn't have to see this."

"Me, too."

"Janet—"

"I know." She read his mind as easily as she did a book these days. "I heard every word of Ty's confession through a speaker. He's very sick, but I don't think he's psychotic. I can't imagine him being a danger to you."

"He isn't. The humiliation he suffered at Annie's hands might just be the thing to make him turn his life around, but I'm not going to waste another second worrying about it."

"No."

"Janet—"

"I know that, too." She smiled before kissing his jaw. "I heard everything that went on in this room. I guess you and I were always so involved in each other that we were the only two people on the planet who didn't know Ty had a reputation for being a liar. I'm just so thankful you found out Lex and Art were always your true friends."

He had to clear his throat. "It means a lot."

"Wade—"

"I know," he whispered against her lips. "We owe some people a huge debt of gratitude."

She nodded. "I think they've left us alone on purpose, but I'm kind of worried about Annie. She put her life on the line for us tonight. That special move of hers could have hurt her and the baby this far along in her pregnancy."

"I'm anxious myself, but Rand's crazy about her. If he suspects there's a problem, he'll have her at the hospital so fast you won't believe it."

"That's true. He's as protective as you are."

"That's because he got a second chance with Annie and knows how lucky he is."

"He told you about that?"

"Yes. We had quite a heart to heart the night I hung out at your condo."

"I'm so thankful for that night."

"Amen," he whispered. "It brought us together. Why don't we go out in back. Right now, I have this urge to be alone with my wife."

Together they moved through the house and onto the patio where the caterers were finishing the cleanup. Wade put his arm around her shoulders and they continued down the steps to the grass.

When they reached the edge of the property, he pulled her against him. "The last time we stood here, I thought my life was over for a second time."

"So did I," she said, her voice trembling.

"Before we thank our hosts, I want to thank you for always loving me. It's the greatest gift a wife could ever give her husband. I've learned so much from you, Janet. There are no words to convey the depth of my love for you. All I can do is show you every minute of every day what you mean to me.

"Now that we've started the family we always wanted, I swear I'll do everything in my power to be the best husband and father I can be. But I'll always need your help. Hold on tight to me, darling."

"I'm holding," she cried softly.

"Never let me go."

"Never!"

EPILOGUE

"ONE more time for the camera, darling."

Janet groaned. It had only been eighteen hours since delivery and she knew she looked a sight. "But you've already taken a whole video of me and the twins." She kissed both adorable heads with their dusting of dark hair.

"I know." Wade grinned. "But these are snaps. I want a picture of my beautiful family to put on the desk at work."

"After you finish, it's my turn to take some of you with the boys. Their little baby faces are so handsome. They look exactly like you, Wade."

"I'm afraid your bias is showing, my love. I concede that James has a little of my look, but David is your mirror image."

She stared up at her husband adoringly. "Can you believe we have two perfect children?"

He flashed her a quick smile that set her heart racing. "We were given help to make up for lost time."

"It's incredible."

"What's really incredible is how beautiful you look. I remember the first time I saw you at the homeless shelter surrounded by the children. Now look at you with two babies of your own."

"Our babies."

"I stand corrected," he murmured huskily. Before

taking a fussy James from her arms, he leaned over to kiss her mouth. "Hmm…I can't wait to do more of that as soon as these little guys have been fed and put back to bed."

"Do you think there will ever be time for 'that' from now on?" Before his smile vanished, she said, "Just kidding."

"What are you trying to do? Give your poor husband a heart attack?"

"No. I'm trying to resign myself to the fact it's going to be a few more weeks before we can make love again. I can't wait," she said breathlessly.

"Neither can I."

"I'm afraid our babies are going to get loved to death in the meantime."

"I'm sure they won't mind."

"I wish there'd be another reunion next year. We could take dozens of pictures to show off the twins."

Wade flashed her a secret smile. "Maybe in nine years we'll have pictures to show off the four of us in Kenya. I'd like our sons to see nature the way we once saw it."

She stared into his eyes. "There's so much life to be lived. Have I told you lately how thankful I am to be living it with you?"

"That makes two of us. Hurry and finish feeding David. I have a need to hold you in my arms for a little while."

"Here on the bed?"

"Where else?"

"Then you'd better put a Do Not Disturb sign on the door."

"I already did, Mrs. Holt. You're in trouble now."

**Don't miss
an exciting opportunity
to save on the purchase of
Harlequin and Silhouette books!**

Buy any two Harlequin or
Silhouette books and save
$10.00 off future Harlequin
and Silhouette purchases

OR

buy any three
Harlequin or Silhouette books
and save **$20.00 off** future
Harlequin and Silhouette purchases.

*Watch for details
coming in October 2000!*

PHQ400

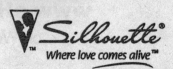

Favorite Harlequin Romance® author

Jessica Steele

brings you

THE MARRIAGE PLEDGE

*For three cousins it has to be marriage—
pure and simple!*

Yancie, Fennia and Astra are cousins
who've grown up together and shared the
same experiences. For all of them, one thing
is certain: they'll never be like their mothers,
having serial meaningless affairs.
It has to be marriage—or nothing!

But things are about to change when three
eligible bachelors walk into their lives....

Titles in this series are:

THE FEISTY FIANCÉE (#3588) in January 2000
BACHELOR IN NEED (#3615) in August 2000
MARRIAGE IN MIND (#3627) in November 2000

*Available in January, August and November wherever
Harlequin Books are sold.*

HARLEQUIN®
Makes any time special.™